Rip to the RESCUE

Rip
to the
RESCUE

Miriam Halahmy

HOLIDAY HOUSE  New York

First Edition

1 3 5 7 9 10 8 6 4 2

Library of Congress Cataloging-in-Publication Data

Names: Halahmy, Miriam, author.

Title: Rip to the rescue / Miriam Halahmy.

Description: First edition. | New York : Holiday House, [2020] | Summary:
    Bullied at school and by his father, thirteen-year-old Jack, a messenger
    boy during the London Blitz, becomes a hero after meeting a stray dog that
    can smell people buried beneath rubble.

Identifiers: LCCN 2019014332 | ISBN 9780823444410 (hardcover)

Subjects: LCSH: Britain, Battle of, Great Britain, 1940—Juvenile fiction. |
    CYAC: Britain, Battle of, Great Britain, 1940—Fiction. | World War,
    1939-1945—Great Britain—Fiction. | Messengers—Fiction. | Rescue
    work—Fiction. | Dogs—Fiction. | London (England)—History—Bombardment,
    1940-1945—Fiction. | Great Britain—History—George VI,
    1936-1952—Fiction.

Classification: LCC PZ7.H12825 Rip 2020 | DDC [Fic]—dc23

LC record available at https://lccn.loc.gov/2019014332

In memory of my grandparents, Joe and Becky,
and their children; Stella, Sylvia, Daphne (my mum),
and Gordon. They lived through the London Blitz.

Contents

We shall fight on the beaches, we shall fight on the landing grounds, we shall fight in the fields and in the streets, we shall fight in the hills;
we shall never surrender.

Winston Churchill's speech, House of Commons, June 4, 1940

— • —

Whistle while you work
Hitler is a twerp
Goering's barmy
so's his army
whistle while you work.

Popular children's song during the Blitz

Rip to the Rescue

1.

Messenger Boy

(SEPTEMBER 1940)

"It's down to you now, Jack," said Warden Yates, scribbling on a report form. "The line's gone dead to the fire station. Get to Skinner Street soon as you can."

Jack and the warden both ducked as a cluster of incendiary bombs exploded across nearby rooftops. Jack could hear shrapnel jingling down the slates like a tune he could almost whistle.

"Close," he muttered, stuffing the message into the pocket of his blue overalls. Then he tightened the strap under his helmet and mounted his bike.

"Keep your head down!" cried the warden as Jack rode off, swerving to avoid the bomb crater at the top of the road.

There was a shop on fire up ahead, lighting up the road in the blackout. Jack raced past as fast as he could, hoping sparks wouldn't set fire to his clothes. That's what happened to Tommy Shepherd last week, and he was still in hospital with serious burns. Tommy was fifteen, almost two years older than Jack. They'd both lied about their ages to get into the messengers. You were supposed to be seventeen.

"What an adventure," Tommy had murmured to him as they stood in line at the Town Hall two months earlier.

Jack was a full head taller than Tommy and the wardens accepted them both into training without a murmur back in July. Now it was the end of September and London had been bombed every night since the seventh.

Even if they found out I was only thirteen, they wouldn't chuck me out, Jack told himself, freewheeling past a pile of rubble. Especially since Tommy got hit.

The thought spurred him on, dreams of making heroic rescues in burning buildings chasing him down the street.

— • —

The Blitz was bad that night. The German bombers were dropping showers of incendiaries all over London, and St. Pancras Station was a target once again. Incendiaries were small, but they were dropped in baskets containing hundreds. The fires they caused lit up the streets like a beacon for the bombers to then drop high explosives. In between, the streets were pitch dark in the blackout made worse by the constant swirl of thick smoke. Jack rode with a wet handkerchief tied around his mouth like a mask to stop breathing in the choking air.

It was bad around Camden, Holborn, and the West End, but Jack knew the East End was getting the worst. A great blanket of smoke sat permanently on the horizon toward the river, and every night the bombers tore into the docks and the homes in the narrow streets. Hundreds were killed, thousands wounded, and the hospitals were so blocked up that the Warden told the boys to use the first-aid post instead.

"If you just need a few stitches, don't go the hospitals, boys. There's them what needs it more."

Jack had been up the top of Parliament Hill fields with Mum to see the damage.

"Those poor people," was all Mum said in a quiet voice.

The wardens said a lot more, and in not such nice language.

"You wouldn't believe it when they drop them high-explosive bombs," Warden Yates had told them. "I was visiting my sister in Bermondsey just as they started on the East End. The air was so wild it pushed and pulled me every which way. I thought my eyeballs would be sucked out my head. Couldn't even get my breath that night, there was smoke like acid all around us. The neighbor's shirt was ripped off by the blast."

"What about our boys on the river?" put in another man. "They had the fireboats pumping water onto the docks, and the fires were so hot the paint blistered on the side of the boats."

"My cousin's crew said the fire leapt the river, burning on both sides. Cranes was crashing over and the whole dock's on fire," another man said. He shook his head and stared at his boots.

Jack wanted to ask what happened to the man's cousin, but he didn't dare.

Warden Yates knocked his pipe out against a wall and said, "All those homes on fire, people staggering around the streets with kiddies—how much more can they take?"

No one answered as they turned back to work.

— • —

Now as Jack rode toward the fire station he concentrated on just getting through in one piece to deliver his message. *Do your job*, he told himself, as he swerved to avoid a shaft of fire swooping down.

He'd never been so needed in all his life.

At the top of Skinner Street the dark was worse than ever. He couldn't see the road at all and slowed down to avoid getting a puncture from broken glass. Hot pieces of shrapnel were falling all around him from the shells fired by anti-aircraft guns. There was a massive thump on his helmet, and a red-hot piece of metal slid down onto the ground. His heart leapt in his chest and he wobbled on his bike, nearly tipping over.

No one was out except a couple of air raid wardens making sure that people had gone down into the bomb shelters.

Suddenly a figure loomed out of the smog, hand up in front of him, crying, "Halt!" He said something else, but the anti-aircraft guns hammering away blocked out the words.

Jack could just make out the tin helmet with WARDEN printed across the front. He pulled down the handkerchief over his mouth and gasped, "Messenger."

"Good lad," the warden shouted and waved him on with the shrouded light of his torch.

Hope he doesn't know Mum and Dad, thought Jack as he set off again. Shrapnel rained back down onto the streets all around him as he pedaled on, his bike skimming through the Blitz.

It wasn't the bombing that scared Jack Castle. He was one of the best riders in the team. The terrifying noise all around didn't bother him either—the only advantage of being deaf in his left ear. It had taken a war for anything good to come of that.

But if Mum and Dad found out, then he'd be in deep trouble. Whatever happened, he had to keep his place in the Messengers secret, especially from Dad.

Just a few more yards, legs pumping like mad, and then he pulled up his brakes and skidded to a halt. Bert Jones and the other men glanced over their shoulders.

"Where is it lad?" barked Bert, his blackened hand stretching out.

"Here. Warden Yates says…"

"All right, all right, give it over." Bert snatched the paper, read it quickly, and snapped, "Harrington Square. Let's go, boys!"

Jack pulled his bike over to the wall as he watched the men leap onto the fire engine and take off, bell ringing, winding their way 'round the cratered road at top speed.

Then he rode back to the wardens' post, avoiding Skinner Street and the fires.

They can't do without me, he thought, smiling to himself as a shower of ash settled like gray snow over the road.

— • —

That's what Warden Yates had told him when he'd volunteered back in July. German bombers were already blowing up RAF planes and ripping through airstrips in southern England.

"You boys will be our life blood, we can't cope without you if truth be told," the air raid warden told Jack and the other messenger boys. "When the real bombing starts and mind you it will—you ain't seen nothing yet—the phone lines will be cut, and we won't be able to communicate with our engines. It's you boys who'll have to bike to the fire stations with messages so we can send the men where they're needed."

It was a hot day and Jack was sweating in the uniform they'd been issued—rubber boots, blue overalls, and a steel helmet—but he didn't care. He was one of the boys at last, not like in school when they called him Deaf Nellie and left him out of everything. In the messengers no one noticed his deaf ear.

Granddad let him keep his kit in the hall cupboard of his flat in an old apple sack. Granddad's memory wasn't that good these days, so it was unlikely he'd tell Mum and Dad. It was a risk Jack had to take, but then the whole war was a risk, wasn't it?

"I can't pretend you'll be safe riding round in the bombing," the warden had said. His eyes narrowed as he looked around at the shining faces. "Speak up now if you want to back out."

No one moved. Jack kept his head lowered.

"You boys," the warden went on, lifting his voice, "you might be too young for soldiering, but you're ready to do your bit for the war effort, eh?"

"Yes sir!" the boys cried out in unison.

Jack pulled himself up to his full height. With his broad shoulders and long legs, the warden would never guess he wasn't yet fourteen. He was taller than two of the other boys, and with a decent bike they weren't going to turn him away.

— • —

By the time Jack returned to the wardens' post, the All Clear was sounding and dawn had broken over the top of St. Pancras Station. The wardens sent them all off, and he pushed his bike home. People had emerged from the shelters by now carrying blankets and thermos flasks. As they stumbled through the rubble and broken glass covering the roads, guiding small children around craters, there was a silent weariness broken only by the occasional cough from the smoke still filling the air.

"I can't stand another night like that," a woman's voice suddenly broke out.

No one said anything, everyone trudged on, faces creased with exhaustion.

Then the shaky voice of an old man called back, "We ain't beaten yet."

Jack watched as they walked by, before riding off. The early morning air was cool after the heat of the blazing night. He'd run a dozen messages, braved another fearsome air raid, and earned a clap on the back from Warden Yates.

I'm *not beaten*, he told himself, as he propped his bike outside Granddad's flat.

— • —

Granddad was already home after the raid, dozing in his armchair. Jack dumped his uniform and went off, arriving back on his street just as Mum and Dad walked into their block of flats.

"Oy, where were you last night?" called out Dad, with a scowl on his face. "I told you I want you down in the shelter when there's a raid. What you doing, sloping off again?"

Jack's shoulders drooped and he shuffled over, pushing his bike.

"Now George, don't get so worked up," said Mum in a soothing voice.

Mum's face was whiter than ever now that it was streaked with dust that had fallen during the raid. Her light brown hair, the same color as Jack's, was coming loose from the bun on her head.

"Give me one good reason why not," snapped Dad, as he brushed some dust off his head.

Dad had fair hair, cropped short all around his head but already thinning on top. Deep lines crisscrossed his pale skin, and he looked older than his forty-two years. Jack's dad had lost a leg in the trenches in the last war and walked with a stick, limping on a badly fitting false leg. Mum said that sometimes Dad's stump hurt quite a bit and blistered, but Dad never mentioned his injury.

He'd also had a "whiff of gas" as the men used to say, and it affected his lungs. He spoke in a gruff, hoarse voice and had terrible coughing fits sometimes. Mum had to wave a newspaper frantically up and down to force air into his lungs.

— • —

But he's always been short tempered, Jack thought now, as he stared at his father's angry face. Yelling at me and Mum for no reason. He's even worse since the war started, as if he's the only one angry with Hitler and his bully boys.

Granddad used to laugh about Dad's short temper growing up. "Got into such a state, that one, over the smallest thing. Always impatient and if he didn't get his own way, he'd stomp out. Not like his brother, your uncle Ken. He were mild as anything. But your dad"—Granddad would shake his head at the memory—"best to leave him alone when he were in a bad mood."

— • —

Jack gave an audible sigh and said, "I biked round to Granddad's. Made sure he was safe. Someone's gotta check on him in the raids."

"See," said Mum, as they started up the stairs. "There's a good lad."

Dad snorted, but to Jack's relief he didn't ask anything else.

Once they'd climbed the three flights to their flat, Dad leaning heavily on the banister and his stick, Mum opened the door and Jack followed her in. Automatically he looked for his cats, Salt and Pepper, and then he remembered. They were gone forever. Even after all these months he still wasn't used to it. That stupid evacuation to Norfolk.

— • —

The whole school had been evacuated just after the war was declared, September 3, 1939, but Jack had no one to pair up with, not like the other lads. He absolutely hated his new home. He was the last boy chosen as they all waited in a village hall in the middle of Norfolk. An old couple took him in. They lived in a tiny hamlet with only three cottages and miles and miles of wet fields and woods. The couple were both deafer than him, and he gave up talking to them by the second night. After three weeks he wrote to Mum and threatened to run away, so she came down to bring him home. She came the next day, and they left on the evening train.

As they arrived back at their flat in Camden, tired and hungry after the long journey, she put a hand on his arm and said, "Sorry, love."

Then she opened the front door. Jack stepped onto the mat and looked down as always, expecting Salt and Pepper to be winding their silky bodies around and around his legs, leaving black and white hairs on his socks, purring in a satisfied way that he was finally home.

But there was no sign of his pets.

"Mum?"

"Speak to your dad," said Mum, her head ducking as she scurried down the hall to the kitchen.

A spear of alarm stabbed his stomach as Jack ran into the living room where Dad was sitting, false leg lying on the carpet, stump up on a footstool covered with the empty trouser leg.

"Where's Salt and Pepper?" demanded Jack.

Dad removed a pipe from his mouth, knocked out the ash into an ashtray, and said, "Now look here. We did what was right, and I don't want to hear no arguments from you, my lad."

"Did what?"

"Like everyone said, the pets will go mad when the bombs start, and we'd never have enough rations to feed one cat, let alone two, so..."

"Where are they then? Who's got them? They're *my* cats. I'm gonna get them back, right now!"

"They're gone," said Dad.

"What do you mean gone?"

"To sleep—the vet put them down. They didn't suffer, so don't go on about it."

— • —

"Put the kettle on, love," called Mum now from the hallway.

"Put it on yourself," growled Jack, his heart heavy, and stomping into his room, he slammed the door shut and threw himself on his bed.

He missed his pets so much. He'd had them since they were tiny kittens, Salt with her pure white fur and Pepper with his black fur sprinkled with gray. They'd stood by him through thick and thin, and no matter how poor his hearing he could always sense when they were talking to him and what they wanted.

Jack looked up at the old familiar cracks in the ceiling. He picked out the one that looked like Salt curled up on a cushion, her distinctive uneven ears sticking up.

"It's all Dad's fault," he whispered to himself. "He's the real enemy."

But there was a taste of gray ash in his mouth as if he'd swallowed a bit of the Blitz fires.

2.

Paula

Two nights later the bombers swung over Camden again as air raid sirens wailed around the streets. Searchlights strafed the night sky and the anti-aircraft guns on Primrose Hill blazed away, hoping to get lucky and bring down a raider.

"I'll go and check on Granddad," cried out Jack, as they all jumped up, Dad grabbing his stick.

Jack was out the door and flying down the three flights of stairs before Dad could stop him, ready for action once more.

Behind him, Dad's hoarse voice grumbled, but Jack only caught a few words in his good right ear.

"When they gon . . . give . . . rest, that's what . . . say."

Jack didn't hear Mum's reply. He was already outside, grabbing his bike, as the courtyard filled up with people racing for shelter.

Wardens were shepherding people forward when a small child suddenly sat down, screaming, and refused to move.

"Oy, pick that kid up!" cried out a warden to the mother, who was also carrying a baby.

The father appeared, picked up the child, and yelling at the exhausted mother, ran forward, a grim look on his face.

Most people were heading for the stations at Camden or Chalk Farm, even though the government had said the underground was not to be used for public shelters. No one trusted the purpose-built shelters because they were above ground. But there was a danger of flooding in the underground if a water main took a direct hit.

Mum was terrified of drowning in the dark. "Your dad would never get out with his leg," she kept saying.

So Dad and Mum went with some of the neighbors to St. Michael's church at the end of the street and sheltered in the freezing-cold crypt. Jack went with them once, but he hated it. He imagined ghosts in all the dark corners.

He preferred being above ground, running messages. *If you thought about all the things that could happen to you in the Blitz, you'd never go outside*, he told himself.

The messenger boys all took the same view.

"No point thinking what you want for Christmas, eh Jack?" Tommy Shepherd had said the week before he got burnt up. "We might not be around, eh?"

They both laughed, but their eyes had locked for a few seconds.

"Graveyard laughter," Warden Yates called it.

— • —

The raiders were heading toward Holborn, Jack decided, as he arrived at Granddad's flat.

"Off out again, Jackie lad," Granddad said in his thin, husky voice, when Jack went into the hallway and opened the cupboard where he kept his uniform. Granddad had once had a head full of blond hair just like Dad, but now it was almost gone, just a stubble of gray down the back and sides.

"Have to," said Jack, pulling his overalls out of the apple sack. "I'm needed."

"So you are, right and proper you should go, just like your dad in the last war."

Jack nodded as he wrestled with his rubber boots. They were a size too small, or he'd grown in the past few weeks.

Granddad wandered off into the kitchen and now called out, "Set the table for tea, George."

George was Dad's name, but Jack knew that Granddad was nearly eighty and often got things muddled.

"Come on, Granddad," Jack said, going into the kitchen and grabbing the old man's arm. "Siren's going off, you gotta get down the shelter, and I have to get to the wardens' post."

As he spoke, Jack was wrapping a coat around Granddad's shoulders and leading him out of the flat into the street.

Spotting a large woman with three children hurrying past, Jack called out, "Can you take Granddad, Mrs. Jenkins? Got to help my dad, he finds it difficult to get about."

Mum and Dad were probably already down in the crypt, but if he told Mrs. Jenkins where he was really going, she'd tell mum, wouldn't she?

"Course I can Jack, love. Charlie, help Mr. Castle—take his arm proper now," she called to a boy about nine years old.

Jack called out his thanks and raced away on his bike. He was the first boy to report for duty and was away within minutes with a message.

He'd been wrong about the bombers targeting Holborn farther west. Bombs were smashing into shops and houses all over Camden.

Skinner Street was one great fog of thick smoke. Jack was about to turn his bike back and choose a different route when a woman emerged right in front of his wheel covered in ash from head to toe, pulling a little girl by the hand.

"This way," cried Jack, jamming on his brakes. He led them to a shelter and watched as they stumbled inside.

"My house, it's all gone," the woman's tearful voice floated back to him as he closed the door.

A bomb exploded so close he nearly jumped out of his skin. For a split second he was tempted to dive into the shelter himself.

But that one didn't have my name on it, he told himself.

He jumped back on his bike and cycled through what seemed like a tunnel of fire, arriving breathless and coughing at the fire station.

"Here, drink this." Bert Jones grabbed him and pushed a water bottle against his lips.

Jack took a couple of gulps and then pulled out his message and handed it over.

"Good lad," said Bert in a gruff voice. "Maybe you should go to the shelter for a while."

Jack shook his head. "Can't do that. We're down a boy. Tommy's still in hospital."

The men had gathered around, and he caught a flicker of approval in their eyes. It felt good to be noticed.

Then Bert yelled, "Euston Road. Come on, lads, look lively!"

They took off, bell ringing, and Jack leaned against the wall for a minute. His lungs felt raw from the fumes, and his legs were shaking a bit. But Granddad's words came into his head as they always did when things were tough. *"Never say die, Jackie lad."*

He sucked back the last of the water, put the bottle down on Bert's shelf, and swung his leg over the saddle. The smoke on

Skinner Street had thinned out a bit, and he pedaled slowly, not wanting to set his cough going again.

Then he heard it—the whir of a falling bomb right overhead. Before he had time to think, a violent explosion threw him from his bike—up, up, and then down again, smashing his body against a broken wall. All the breath went from his lungs; a searing pain sliced through his head and another down his arm. Dazed, he pushed himself onto all fours, but his eyes were watering so much from the smoke he couldn't see anything.

Someone was helping him to his feet, saying something Jack couldn't make out. Both ears seemed to have gone deaf now in the blast. *What if I never hear again?* he thought, as he swayed against the figure. His eyes were smarting from the smoke, but he thought it was a boy who'd come to his rescue, smaller than him but quite strong, he decided.

His good ear began to clear, and he heard the boy say, "Nearly there. Watch out for the steps."

He pulled open a door and lead Jack down. One eye cleared enough to see they were in cellars beneath some shops. It was full to bursting, but the boy found a tiny space. "Sit down here, you must be feeling dizzy."

Jack tried to nod but that made the room spin.

There was the crump of a bomb overhead, and everyone ducked. A child let out a high-pitched scream, and plaster came down on a group of men huddled over an upturned crate playing dominoes. They didn't even look up, just brushed the dust away and continued playing.

Jack collapsed on the floor as the boy called out, "Is there a doctor in here? This boy's bleeding badly."

A hubbub started up all around as people called back.

"Doctor? We ain't got nothing like that in this shelter, mate."

"You want Buckingham Palace, lovey, this is scummy Camden, no doctors down 'ere."

Then a warden was pushing people aside, calling out, "All right, all right, that's enough. Stop that racket you lot and give the lad some air."

He dropped down to one knee and, pulling bandages from his bag, said, "Anyone got any water? The lad's all cut up. One of Warden Yates's messenger boys, ain't you?"

Jack nodded.

The tone of the crowd changed.

"Proper little hero, ain't he," said a man in his pajamas, clutching a hot-water bottle.

"One of them got all burnt up last week, you know, Tommy Shepherd what lives over the fish shop," someone else said, his hands full with a large clock, a thermos flask, and a footstool.

Everyone was staring down at Jack now, and a woman with a baby said, "God bless you, love."

Jack's head was thumping and there seemed to be blood everywhere. *Mine*, he wondered, *or the other boy's?*

Someone offered a water bottle, and the warden cleaned his cuts and bandaged his head and arm. "Soon as the All Clear sounds, you get yourself off to the first-aid post on Euston Road. Need stitches in those cuts, I reckon. Where's your girlfriend?"

"What girl?" mumbled Jack, puzzled.

Then a now-familiar voice said, "Don't worry. I'll look after him."

Looking up, Jack saw a girl about twelve years old, with dark brown hair cut in a bob. She was several inches shorter than him with narrow shoulders and a slight frame. The girl had olive skin and dark eyes that seemed to blaze with anger. She wore cotton trousers, lace-up black shoes, and what looked like a soldier's khaki battle jacket, with big pockets on the chest and an insignia on the sleeve.

He gave the girl a nod. "I'm Jack," he said. "Thanks for rescuing me."

"Paula. I forgot my first-aid kit." She frowned as if she couldn't tolerate such stupidity.

"I don't even carry a bandage," said Jack with a grin that made him wince as pain shot through his head.

"My dad's an emergency room doctor, so I know about Blitz injuries," said Paula. She had a flat, almost monotone way of speaking.

"Well, your dad's a blimmin' hero too, ain't he?" said the woman with a baby.

"Hmm," grunted the warden, struggling to his feet. "That's all very well, young lady, but when the sirens go you need to get straight down the shelter. Or better still, why ain't you evacuated?"

Jack and Paula exchanged looks, and in that instant Jack knew she didn't care any more about the Blitz than he did. *But why not?* he wondered.

"Mum needs me at home," said Paula.

"Well, she needs you to stay alive, don't she?" said the warden in a gruff voice. "Anyways, this boy here, he's a valuable part of the war effort, and you just saved his life."

Jack felt his chest swell with pride, and the girl brushed a lock of hair from her forehead.

She hasn't even noticed my deaf ear, he told himself.

3.

"You Weren't in the Trenches!"

"You can lean on me if you like," said Paula, taking Jack's arm as they emerged from the shelter.

Jack's head spun a little. "Might be a good idea," he said. "This way." He nodded forward.

The All Clear was still sounding in the streets. The air was thick with brick dust and the smell of cordite from the bombs. Houses had been sliced down the front, and Jack could see right into bedrooms and bathrooms, wallpaper hanging down in strips and mirrors shattered like spiderwebs. It didn't seem right somehow, as though they were peeking through someone's curtains and raking through their private lives.

Up ahead, a woman pulled aside broken planks of wood as she climbed over bricks; and then she cried out, "It's here! Look Harry."

A man clambered up behind her and, shaking his head, said in a booming voice, "Well I never, not a stick of furniture left standing, but your bloomin' china survives in one bloomin' piece."

— • —

Crowds were pouring out of Chalk Farm Station, trudging home dazed and exhausted after another night sleeping on the platforms, all squashed up together.

Someone was pushing a bicycle, and Jack wondered what had happened to his bike. He couldn't remember where he'd been when the bomb exploded. Was it Skinner Street or beyond? He shook his head and a sharp pain made him woozy for a second.

"Hang on," said Paula, gripping him more tightly. "Dad always says you must stay awake if you get a head injury. You're not going to fall asleep, are you?"

"No," grunted Jack, but all he really wanted to do was lie down and close his eyes.

They plodded on, and the crowds started to thin as they reached the first-aid post. There were so many wounded they were lined up on the street, waiting patiently to be seen.

"Maybe we should go to the hospital," said Paula. "Find my dad. He'll patch you up."

"The hospitals are for those who can't walk," said Jack.

After about an hour, they found a place on a wooden bench

inside the building. Jack closed his eyes for a few minutes, and then Paula was shaking him awake.

"Doctor's here, Jack. Wake up now."

A tired-looking doctor checked Jack's wounds. "Not too bad," he said, swabbing the cuts.

The antiseptic stung so much it was all Jack could do to stop tears coming to his eyes.

Behind him people were talking about the raid last night. One man said in a loud voice, "And you know the Wilsons what live down Canning Road? Their kiddie got rescued all right, but he's gone and lost a leg. Only eight, ain't he?"

"Terrible," said another man. "Something shocking. They need to go over and stop that Mr. Hitler in his bloomin' tracks."

"Tried that in France, didn't they, and look what happened? Dunkirk and the whole bloomin' army trapped," someone else chipped in. "Took hundreds just to rescue them."

People muttered and grumbled around them as the doctor worked away on Jack's wounds, stitching his head and arm and putting bandages around both.

"Come back in five days to have the stitches taken out," said the doctor, getting up. "Keep that arm in the sling."

Then he turned to the next patient, a three-year-old boy with glass in his eye.

As they walked away from the hospital, Paula said, "I can see you home if you like."

Jack didn't really want to go home. Dad would see from his wounds that he'd been out in the Blitz and not down a shelter. He'd be furious. Anyway, he needed to change out of his overalls.

"My granddad lives nearby. He'll make us a cup of tea."

"Fine," said Paula.

— • —

"Didn't know they had girls in the army," said Granddad once they were all settled with a pot of tea between them.

Paula glanced down at the battle jacket and, taking a spoon of sugar, stirred her cup around and around. Then she said in her flat voice, "It belonged to my brother—he was wounded at Dunkirk. They got him back to Dover but he died in hospital."

Jack eyes widened as stared at the girl. A dead brother. Maybe that's why her voice sounded like she'd squashed down all feelings.

The silence became more and more uncomfortable until Jack forced himself to ask, "How old was your brother?"

"Nineteen. Me and my sister were brought over from Devon where we'd been evacuated to see him before..." She stopped and they all stared deep into their tea cups. "I took his jacket and this."

In one swift movement Paula undid the button over the left pocket in the jacket, pulled out a whistle and blew out the Morse code for SOS.

Jack watched, puzzled.

"Like a Boy Scout," said Paula, her burning eyes wide, "I'm always prepared."

"For what?" said Jack.

"The invasion."

He gave her a surprised look. "We don't know for certain Hitler will invade us. He didn't cross the Channel after Dunkirk, did he? Everyone said that was his big chance and he blew it."

"It'll happen," said Paula raising her voice. "And when the Germans get here, I'll have to defend my family. I'm the eldest now."

Paula's words sent a chill through Jack. It was as though she knew something no one else did.

Was her dad really a doctor, or did he work for the government? he wondered. Maybe he's a spy.

"Well I don't know," muttered Granddad to himself, shuffling the sugar bowl around. "Keep my spoons in the kitchen drawer, Germans or no Germans."

Jack could see he was beginning to wander as usual.

Then Granddad barked, "What does your mum say about you wearing an army jacket!"

"I don't think that's our business, Granddad," said Jack, going red.

Paula shrugged. "The grownups don't notice anything since

Joe. Mum volunteers all night with bombed-out families, and Dad's always at the hospital."

"What school do you go to?" said Jack.

"It was wrecked on the first day of the Blitz," said Paula.

Jack laughed. "Like mine."

"Me and my sister, Becky—she's eleven, just over a year younger than me—we're supposed to have lessons with our big cousin, Gerda," Paula went on, "but we know how to give her the slip."

For the first time, Paula gave Jack the ghost of a grin.

He grinned back.

"Weren't you evacuated?" she asked Jack.

"Don't ask about the cats!" said Granddad, waving his hand and knocking into the milk bottle.

"Whoa, take it easy," said Jack, grabbing the bottle before it tipped all over the floor.

"Lovely little things they was," muttered Granddad.

"What happened to the cats?" asked Paula.

So Jack told her the whole story as Granddad frowned and muttered.

"And your dad said he had them put down because they couldn't feed cats on the rationing?" asked Paula when Jack had finished.

"Yes. But Mum said later she could have found food for Salt and Pepper."

"That's not very fair," said Paula. "What do they think about you being a messenger, biking around in the Blitz?"

"They don't know. I keep my uniform here," said Jack, glancing over at Granddad.

Paula nodded to Granddad, "So you understand about Jack and his war work."

Granddad looked confused and Jack said, "Granddad understands, just not everything, you know."

Paula's face softened and she nodded. "I get it."

Jack wiped a hand across his face. His wounds were throbbing, and he didn't want to be caught out in an air raid again. "I'd better be getting home. How about you?"

"I'll walk you home first."

— • —

They settled Granddad in his armchair and then walked around to Jack's flat.

When Mum opened the door she cried out, "What happened? Jack, my goodness, oh dear."

She pulled them into the living room where Dad was resting, false leg on the floor as usual. Jack glanced at Paula but she didn't seem bothered. Mum pushed Jack into an armchair, but Paula hovered in the doorway.

Before Mum could offer her a seat, Dad grabbed his stick and crashed it down on the coffee table. His cup leapt up off the saucer and flew into the hearth, shattering into small pieces.

Paula let out a gasp and pressed herself against the door.

Jack felt himself go red. What must she think of his family?

"George!" cried out Mum.

"Don't you George me! Look at that boy!" he blasted out, as Mum dropped to her knees, clearing up the mess.

"George, please. We have a visitor," murmured Mum.

Dad ignored her. Eyes blazing, he waved his stick at Jack and snarled, "You got yourself caught in a raid! Think you're invincible, don't you? You should've been in the trenches, then you'd know what a real war can do!"

"George! Give the lad a chance to—"

But Dad wasn't listening as he steamed on. "I've a good mind to send you back to Norfolk, my lad. You're too young to be trusted in the bombing. And why are you still in London, my girl!" Dad turned to Paula, his face white with anger.

"My mum needs me since my brother was killed," said Paula in her flat voice. Two red points appeared in her cheeks and she wouldn't meet Jack's eye. "I'd better go," she muttered.

Then she turned on her heel and went out, closing the front door behind her with a firm click.

"What a little madam," finished Dad, and he shifted his stump on the stool.

Jack was shaking with anger, but he blurted out, "I'm sick of you treating me like a kid. Showing me up in front of my friends."

"Don't answer me back!" Dad yelled.

"Please, George," said Mum in a helpless voice.

"That boy needs to learn some manners, and where's my tea?" was all Dad said, slumping back in his chair, his voice even more hoarse than usual.

Jack exchanged looks with Mum. Why doesn't she stand up to him? He treats her like a slave, always clearing up his mess. He's such a bully.

But Mum just dropped her eyes as usual.

There was nothing else to say. Jack stomped off to his bedroom, shut the door, and threw himself down on his bed.

You might think you're the big hero out in the Blitz, Jack Castle, he told himself, *but you're never going to stand up to your dad, are you?*

Maybe I should go and live with Granddad, was his last thought before he fell into a troubled sleep.

4.

Demolition Gang

When Jack woke up the next day, it was almost lunchtime. He could hear voices at the front door. Then a clearer voice said, "Is he feeling better?"

It was Paula. Jack sat up, his head spinning, and called out, "Wait a minute!"

There was a silence. Jack heard footsteps in the hallway. He pulled on a sweater and trousers and went out of the bedroom.

Mum and Paula were in the kitchen.

Mum was pouring tea. "The sugar ration's run out dear, sorry," she was saying.

"I don't take sugar," said Paula, giving Jack a nod as he came in.

Jack nodded back and said, "Dad gone?"

"Yes, love," said Mum in a bright voice. "Jack's dad works at the printers," she said to Paula. "Nice sitting-down job which suits, you know, the leg. He lost it in the trenches and it gives him ever such a lot of trouble, don't it Jack?"

Jack glared back.

"I've got something of yours," said Paula, as Mum turned to the sink.

Bike, she mouthed.

"Oh, right," said Jack. "Finish your tea. We'd better go."

Paula gulped her tea down, and as she headed for the front door, Mum grabbed Jack's arm and held him back. "Don't be too rough on your dad, eh Jack?"

Jack didn't want Paula listening in. "See you outside," he called as she disappeared.

"I can always go and live with Granddad if he doesn't want me here anymore," he said.

Mum's eyes filled with tears. "No Jack, please."

"Don't see why not."

But he couldn't meet her eye.

Mum relied on him to do all the heavy jobs these days. Like bringing the shopping up the three flights of stairs to their flat. He knew Dad found it hard to help with things like that, but it wasn't Mum's fault he was so miserable and petty all the time. Mum wiped her eyes on her apron.

Jack heaved a sigh and said, "Course I'll stay. I won't let you down, Mum."

"There's a good boy," she murmured, with a watery smile.

A warm glow went up through him as he went off. *At least Mum still cares about me.*

If anyone behaves like a kid, it's Dad, he fumed to himself as he ran down the three flights of stairs.

— • —

It hadn't always been like that. Dad was short tempered and his war injuries didn't help, as Mum had told Jack since he was little. But Dad never complained about the pain or the coughing. Granddad was always saying how stoic Dad was. "Came home from the trenches and just got on with it. What you'd expect, of course," Granddad would say, and Jack couldn't help admiring that.

But Dad's temper had become so much worse since the war started, especially in the last few weeks with the London Blitz and all the bombing. *It was quite strange really*, Jack thought. Dad would suddenly fly into a huge rage, like when Paula came around, lashing out with his stick. More than once he'd nearly swiped Jack across the legs.

Everyone's sick of the bombing, Jack told himself. *Why does he think he's got the right to be so angry all the time?*

Mum kept making excuses, but Jack was fed up with hearing them.

I'm a man now, Jack told himself. *I've been wounded in the*

Blitz. I'm needed for the war effort. It's my Dad who's the useless one.

— • —

"Here's your bike." Paula broke into his thoughts as he went into a side passage. "I didn't ride it here," she went on. "It's too high for me, but I think it's just fine."

"Thanks. I'm going to see the air raid wardens, tell them what happened. Coming?"

"All right."

Paula grabbed the bike, and they set off.

Jack was still feeling a bit dizzy as they strolled along the road to the wardens' post.

Warden Yates was very sympathetic, but his face was lined with worry as he said, "We're down another boy too. Dennis was hit in the raid last night. In hospital with two broken legs. A right bad night it were all round."

"I'll be back," said Jack. "Soon as my stitches are out."

The warden's face lightened. "That's the spirit," he said, clapping him on the back.

"He thinks a lot of you," said Paula, as they walked off.

She kept hold of the bike, and Jack didn't object.

"I'm supposed to be out in the Blitz, it's my job," said Jack. "But what on earth were you doing wandering around in a raid? You'll get yourself killed liked that."

If there was an invasion, thought Jack glancing at the girl, *she's hardly big enough to stand up for herself. That battle jacket won't save her.*

"I was on my way to the shelter," said Paula.

She paused as they picked their way around a large crater in the pavement.

Beyond the crater, Paula went on, "I stopped to look up and saw a raider open his bomb doors and bombs fell through the sky. I couldn't take my eyes away. But a boiling bit of shrapnel fell past my cheek and singed my hair. It was a bit stupid standing out there, I suppose."

"Very stupid! You can't stand around in a raid, anything could happen," said Jack, furrowing his eyebrows. "You should be in the shelters."

Paula's shoulders hunched up, and she crouched down over the handlebars, closing back inside herself. Used to silence himself, Jack walked on beside her.

When they arrived at Granddad's flat, they propped the bike in the hallway. Jack went into the living room. Granddad was dozing in his armchair. Satisfied, Jack left him in peace.

Back outside, Paula was leaning against a wall, arms folded. But she raised her eyebrows at him as if to say, *What now?*

"We could go crater-goggling, as Mum says after a raid," said Jack, with a grin.

Paula nodded.

"Come on then."

Anything was better than going back home.

As they got near to the canal flowing under Camden High Street, a voice shouted from a bombed house, "Hey messenger boy! Heard you got all blitzed up!"

It was Alf Edwards, known as Rocky by his gang. Jack knew them all from school and his heart sank. Rocky was already fourteen, taller than Jack and bigger all around. He had wavy black hair, reddish sunburnt skin as though he was never indoors, and a reputation for never being beaten in a fight. No one crossed Rocky. In school he'd ruled the playground. It was Rocky who gave Jack the nickname Deaf Nellie.

Jack didn't want Paula to see he was scared, so he threw back his shoulders and called back, "How'd you know I got hit?"

"My dad's an air raid warden," said Rocky. He was standing astride a pile of rubble, hands on his hips like a general surveying his army. "How many stitches?"

"Sixteen."

"That ain't nothing," called back Ned, with a snort.

Ned was still only twelve, much shorter and thinner than Rocky. He was all bony corners, and Jack had often felt a bruising poke in the ribs. Ned's head was shaved, and his clothes were ragged and torn. There was a mocking look on his thin face, white as ceiling dust.

Ned was the school thief. He'd swiped Jack's new pencils

from his bag one morning last year. They'd been a Christmas present from Granddad, but Ned denied it to his face and threatened to punch his teeth down his throat. Later he saw Ned sell the pencils for threepence to another boy in the playground, but Jack was too scared to stand up to him.

I'm a messenger boy now, Jack told himself, but some of the old fear hovered around him still.

"Let's go," he muttered to Paula. "I know them from school, they're … you know."

Paula shrugged and started to walk away, but Rocky called down in his cool voice, "Come and join us if you ain't got nothing else to do."

"Doing what?" asked Paula, staring around the bomb site.

"Looking for souvenirs," said another boy as he held up a gleaming bullet. "It's live."

"Better be careful with that," said Paula.

Rocky held out his hand, and the boy gave him the bullet. He examined it carefully. "What do you know?" he said to Paula.

"When I was evacuated a farmer taught me to shoot a bit," she answered.

Mutters of respect went around the gang.

"All good shots welcome here," said Rocky, giving Paula a dazzling smile.

To Jack's amazement, Paula's cheeks went bright red and she tucked her hair behind her ears.

So what's that all about? he wondered. *Maybe I should just push off and leave them to it.* But something in Rocky's face, grinning down at him, made him hesitate.

Maybe things are different now he'd been wounded, and he wouldn't mind showing that sniveling jerk Ned a thing or two.

Rocky raised his arm again and pronounced, "Come on boys, you know what Churchill said, 'We'll fight on the beaches—'"

"And in the toilets!" yelled another boy, picking up a toilet seat and throwing it through a broken window.

"Go to it lads," cried out Rocky. "For King and Country!"

Whoops went up as the gang attacked what was left of the house, hurling stones at broken windows and bashing away at crumbling walls.

Paula sat down on an upturned crate, glancing at Rocky out of the corner of her eye.

She's not in a hurry to go, thought Jack.

Rocky picked up a hammer, jumped down from the rubble, and handed it to Jack. He nodded at a half-broken sink lying on the ground.

Jack hesitated, and then he took the hammer in his good hand, raised it above his head, and brought it crashing down on the sink again and again until nothing was left but a pile of broken shards. It felt so good to be the one in charge for once, instead of biking through the streets while the bombers decided your fate. It was as though Rocky and his gang were taking back control from the Luftwaffe.

About time too, thought Jack. His hair was plastered to his scalp and the sling was covered with brick dust, but he didn't care.

He looked around at Paula. Maybe her way of taking control was to take her dead brother's place, wearing his jacket and practicing Morse code on that dented tin whistle.

He was just about to call out when a voice shrilled, "Can I play?"

A girl about eleven years old stood on the street. She was wearing a short dress, white socks, and scuffed sandals. She had long, sturdy-looking legs and brown curly hair, which she flicked back over her shoulders as she spoke. Her skin was the color of golden sand, and the friendly grin on her face made Jack grin back.

"Hiya, Becks," called out Ned to Jack's surprise.

He watched as Ned clambered down from the bomb site, shoved his hands in his torn pockets, and walked over to the girl. "What's new?"

"Who's this, Becky?" asked Paula. "She's my sister," Paula explained to Jack; and turning back to the girl, she said in a sharp voice, "How do you know these boys?"

"I only know Ned," said Becky, her dark eyes wide. "We play cricket with the kids in his yard. Over there." She pointed toward a tenement block looming over the canal. "I'm really good at fielding. I'm quick and I can catch."

Jack stared in disbelief as Ned said, "Yep, the best."

Becky gave Paula a smirk. "See?" she said.

Paula glared back.

"You'll get yourself dirty over here, nipper," called out one of the gang. "Better get home to mummy." He gave a snigger, and a couple of the boys joined in.

Ned leapt forward, fists up, shouting, "Mind your manners, you dopes!"

"Calm down, mate," said Rocky, and he swung down to the pavement on a length of electric cable—*just like Tarzan*, thought Jack.

Ned lowered his fists and went over to chat with Becky, who laughed out loud at everything he said.

Jack lowered his hammer and watched as Rocky leaned on the wall next to Paula. "Come over anytime," he said. "We can always use a munitions expert."

He gave her his dazzling smile, and Paula's cheeks went red again.

I don't fit in with this lot, thought Jack, with an inward sigh. *Just like when I was at school.*

He was about to leave when Becky said, "Peppermint, anyone?" She offered Jack the bag first.

He'd look stupid if he went off in a sulk now, so he took one and muttered his thanks.

Ned grabbed the bag and stuffed three in his mouth.

"I really miss sweets, don't you, Ned?" said Becky.

Her dad's a doctor, and Ned's a crook from the tenements, thought Jack. *Can't she see through him?*

"I can get you sweets anytime," said Ned. "What do you want?"

"Milk chocolate," said Becky with a sigh.

Jack murmured in Paula's ear, "The only way he'll get sweets is by nicking them."

Paula's eyes narrowed and she slipped the whistle, which she'd been turning over in her hand, back into her pocket. Then she stepped away from the wall and said, "Come on, Becky. Mum wants us home before it gets dark."

"Oh, yes," said Becky. "It's Friday, we have to get ready for Shabbo—"

"Shut UP!" Paula screamed in Becky's face.

Becky's hand flew up to her mouth. "Sorry Paula." Her eyes welled with tears. "I forgot."

Paula grabbed her sister's hand and pulled her off down the street.

"See you," called out Jack.

Paula stopped and turned, still gripping Becky's hand. There was a frown on her face.

But not anger, thought Jack. *More like fear. What's spooked her?*

Then Paula called back in her flat voice, "Come over sometime. Opposite Primrose Hill, Number twenty-eight, the house with the blue door."

Pleased to be invited, Jack drew himself up to his full height and nodded. He watched the girls as they turned the corner opposite Chalk Farm Station.

Glancing over his shoulder at Rocky, their eyes met, and Rocky gave a cool nod.

That's all right, then, thought Jack as he set off back down the High Street. *I'm not that little deaf kid anymore, bullied at school. Rocky, and his gang, respects me. I've even got war wounds.*

He couldn't wait to show off his scars.

5.

A Starving Dog

As Jack walked back toward Camden Town, the air raid sirens sounded. People started to run to the underground station, and caught up in the rush, Jack found himself on the stairs being swept down by the crowd to the platform, which was already filling up.

He pushed his way along until he found an unoccupied bench and claimed it. Then craning his neck, he spotted Mrs. Jenkins with her children including her oldest boy, Charlie, who was gripping Granddad's arm.

"Over here, Charlie," he called out. "I've grabbed a bench."

Charlie pushed through the crowd and they managed to sit Granddad down, his back leaning against the wall.

"Ain't they supposed to come at night, Jackie lad?" grumbled Granddad.

"They must have slipped the radar down at the coast," said Jack, taking off his coat and wrapping it around Granddad's shoulders. "Our boys will be after them soon enough. I don't think it'll be a long raid."

The platform was filling up and people were vying for places to set down all their belongings: blankets and baskets of food and even pets, though the government had said dogs weren't allowed in the shelters.

Kids raced up and down playing fighter pilots and veering dangerously close to the edge. Jack knew the trains didn't stop in a raid. If any of the kids fell on the tracks, they'd be crushed to death, or electrocuted.

The family next to Jack had brought flasks of tea and packets of sandwiches.

He realized he was starving as his stomach started to rumble.

"Here we go, Jack," said Mrs. Jenkins, her plump red arms dipping up and down as she organized their spot. "Nice cuppa and a biscuit for Mr. Castle, and you help yourself now. Need to keep your strength up with those wounds, like."

Mrs. Jenkins was unwrapping food and taking out a huge flask from a basket she had set down on the platform. Settled on the bench next to Granddad, she handed out refreshments to her little group, including an elderly man who seemed to be all alone, sitting on the platform like a little island in the middle of the swelling crowd.

"That's Morrie Atkins," said Mrs. Jenkins to Jack as he munched on a jam sandwich. "Lost his wife on the first day; incendiary set fire to the house. She couldn't get out in time. Morrie was visiting a neighbor. Came back, and there weren't nothing left to bury." She shook her head.

Jack stared at the old man and a shiver went through him. *I'll never leave Granddad alone to fend for himself,* he thought.

But a little voice in his head said, *Well,* you'd *better not get hit again, eh?*

The crump of the bombs seemed right overhead, and flurries of dust came down from the ceilings. Jack saw a mouse run across the tracks; two little boys laid bets that they could catch it.

No chance they'll be allowed down there, thought Jack with an amused smile.

It's filthy down here, he thought, *and we're all trapped like rats in a cellar. Just what Hitler wants.* He thought of Paula and her angry eyes flashing when she told them about her brother. *We're all angry,* he thought, *but I just want to get on with my job. Hope these cuts heal very soon and I can get back to running messages.* He hated being squashed on the platform with half of Camden.

Card games were laid out and some grownups started singing a song, shouting out the chorus, "Run rabbit, run rabbit, run, run, run; Bang, bang, bang, bang goes the farmer's gun."

Charlie Jenkins shrieked, "BANG!" so loudly, his mother gave him a clip around the ear.

"Ow! Mu-um!" Charlie shrieked even louder, rubbing his ear.

"Now stop scaring everyone," she shouted back.

Suddenly a warden appeared, blowing his whistle. "Right, that's it, you lot," he bellowed as everyone looked his way. "All Clear just sounded, get off back to your homes."

"Not much point," a man called out, a child on his hip. "We'll only have to come back tonight."

People called out in agreement, but the warden shook his head and said, "Come on, look lively, and don't be so ruddy miserable."

Jack was relieved as he helped Granddad out of the underground, a long slow process as hundreds of people slowly climbed the stairs. Up in the fresh evening air, Jack took some deep breaths.

"I hate it down there," he said as they walked off.

"Me too, Jackie lad, but I hate the bombers even more," Granddad said. "You go off now; I'll be all right with Charlie."

The younger boy was beside them, and he linked arms with Granddad. Jack watched them go.

I'd better go home and see if Mum needs anything, he told himself, but he wasn't looking forward to seeing Dad again.

He was about to cross the road toward his flats when he heard a scrabbling sound behind a broken wall. Peering over, he saw a dog, one ear torn, tongue lolling out of the side of his mouth. His fur was a mixture of brown and black, but around one eye was a large reddish patch that gave him a lopsided, daft look.

The dog was shivering as he fixed his huge brown eyes on Jack. Then he hunkered down, crept forward, and licked Jack's shoe.

Jack could see how thin and scrawny he was, his shoulder bones sticking up through the matted fur. His heart went out to the starving animal.

"Here, boy." He pulled the last bit of Mrs. Jenkins'sandwiches out of his pocket and offered it. The dog snatched it and swallowed it whole.

Jack was about to walk away when he suddenly imagined his beloved Salt and Pepper out in the streets, all alone. How awful if they had to dodge bombs, poor little cats, starving, hungry, and no one to care for them.

As he hesitated, the dog raised his head and came up to stand quietly beside him. Jack took a few steps forward...and the dog followed.

"What do you want, boy?"

The dog gazed back with his daft look, tongue lolling.

Dogs are man's best friend, Jack told himself. *I could keep him at Granddad's for a bit; just until I find someone to take him. It'll be all right so long as Dad doesn't find out.*

"Will you behave for Granddad?" he said, stroking the rough fur along the dog's neck.

The dog seemed to prick up his good ear.

"Come along then."

He walked off, the dog trotting by his side as if they had been best friends forever.

— • —

Granddad was delighted. "There's a good boy, ain't you, a right good boy," he kept saying.

The dog sat up on his haunches, panting and giving little whining sounds until Granddad fed him his entire bacon ration for the week.

"You can't give him all your food," said Jack, pulling the dog over to an old sack he'd laid out on the kitchen floor. "Lie down here, come on," he said, pointing to the sack.

The dog obeyed, settling down, his nose resting on his legs stretched out in front, one eye half closed, the other keeping a hopeful lookout for more food.

Granddad rummaged through his cupboards, pulling out tins. "He could have spam for dinner, couldn't he Jackie lad?"

Jack gave a sigh. "I suppose so. The main thing is not to let Mum and Dad see him. I'll see if I can find a proper home for him tomorrow. And if there's an air raid, lock him up in the flat."

Jack left them to it and walked back home. It was already seven. Dad and Mum had finished dinner and were listening to the radio in the living room.

Jack ate alone in the kitchen and went to bed early, his wounds aching after the long day.

6.

Keep a Low Profile

Jack woke early on Saturday morning, refreshed after a whole night without a raid. His first thought was, *No work today, so Dad's at home.*

That decided it. He'd go and see the dog now. Granddad was bound to be awake.

Slipping out quietly, he made his way through the streets to Granddad's flat. He arrived to find that the dog had made a terrible mess on the floor. Granddad was leaning against the kitchen sink shaking his head.

"I don't think spam did Rip any good," muttered Granddad.

"Rip? Is that his name?" Jack said with a grin.

"Got a ripped ear, ain't he? Been in a fight and come off worse, I reckon."

Jack put the kettle on, then cleaned the smelly floor.

Once they'd all had some tea and toast, he said, "Well, Rip, if that's your name...."

The dog sat up on his haunches, his dark eyes fixed on Jack.

"He likes it," said Granddad.

Jack nodded. "Come on, let's get some fresh air."

Rip sprang up and trotted to his side, and Jack reached down to pat his back. The dog's musky smell and warm, rough fur already felt familiar, as though he had his own proper pet again.

Might be just for a couple of days, he told himself. *He can't stay here. But we can be friends for now, can't we?*

They left Granddad buttering the last slice of toast and set off toward the canal.

As they walked past the canal, the remains of an autumn mist lingered over the water; but the sun was already bright and would soon burn it off. If he didn't look across at the bombed-out buildings, Jack could almost imagine it was just another autumn day in September with school on Monday morning.

Do I want the war to end? thought Jack, watching as a long canal boat slid past. *Who would I be if I wasn't in the messengers?*

He was already missing the action and the thrill of biking through the Blitz.

Rip was nosing around some litter on the railway bridge. On the other side was the road up to Primrose Hill.

Jack whistled and the dog looked up, pricking his good ear. "Come on, Rip, let's go and see if Paula and Becky are out early."

He broke into a jog, and the dog fell in beside him. They went over the railway bridge and toward the hill, which loomed up in front of them. On top were anti-aircraft guns that thundered every night. The houses alongside the park were huge, four or five floors high with cellars and attics.

Jack was looking for a blue door when a voice called, "Hey! Who goes there?"

Looking up, he saw Becky hanging out of a first-floor window, her curly hair blowing around her face.

"Hi!" he called back with a grin, patting Rip.

"What a lovely dog! I'm coming down. Wait there!"

A minute later a door opened, and Becky ran down to the garden gate. "Come in, Mummy says you can have breakfast with us. What's your dog's name?"

"Rip."

"Oh, because of his poor torn ear."

Becky led the way through the front door, which Jack could see was dark blue, and along a passage to a big sunny kitchen. There was a sink in the middle of a long counter and a kettle whistling on the stove.

He spotted Paula grabbing two silver candlesticks from the kitchen table and putting them on a counter, pushing them to the back, almost as if she didn't want him to notice. Candle wax had dripped down the sides, and he wondered if they lit candles for dinner. *That's fancy*, he thought.

A breadboard with a braided loaf on it stood on the large wooden table.

"Hope you're hungry," Paula said. She nodded to a man sitting at the table. "Dad, this is Jack."

A stocky man with thinning gray hair, thick-rimmed glasses, and a deep scar on his forehead—*Shrapnel scar*, thought Jack, *from the trenches?*—was sitting at the table.

"Doctor Goodman," said the man in a tired voice. "But please call me Ted. This is my wife, Rose."

He waved a hand toward a short, slender woman in an apron, drying dishes. She had the same curly hair as Becky and the same olive skin as the girls. Deep lines ran down either side of her mouth, but she gave Jack a kind smile.

"Sit down, please, Jack," Rose said. "Paula, call Gerda. Becky, give Jack some cutlery."

"Thank you," said Jack, pulling out a chair and sitting down.

Rose started to break eggs into a frying pan. The doctor cut thick slices from the plaited loaf. Jack could see the crust had a golden sheen. It looked delicious.

"There you are," said Becky as she clattered cutlery next to Jack's plate. "I've polished it a million times so you can see your face in it." She tossed her curls and grinned at him.

"I'm impressed," he said, as Paula returned with a young woman in her early twenties.

"This is Cousin Gerda," said Paula.

Gerda was taller than Rose, with long, thin arms and legs and her dusty brown hair in a tight bun. She wore a gray skirt and a knitted cardigan. Her face was so pale it was almost translucent, and there were dark shadows under eyes that flickered nervously around the room.

"She's actually a rather distant cousin," said Becky, sitting next to Jack and calling Rip over to her side.

"Don't be so rude," said Paula, with a frown.

"Behave girls," said Rose, flicking her tea cloth toward the sisters as they glared at each other.

"It's a bit mad in here," said the doctor to Jack with a grin, as he dropped two thick slices of bread onto his plate.

— • —

Rose dished up eggs and poured tea. The braided loaf quickly disappeared, and Rose brought out some freshly baked rolls. The jam was homemade, and there was also a thick wedge of cheese, which Becky fed in chunks to the ever-starving Rip.

Between mouthfuls, Jack had to answer a barrage of questions mainly from Becky about finding Rip and where he was going to keep him.

"Not at home," said Jack, wiping the egg yolk up with bread. He only dared do it because he saw the doctor do the same. "My

Dad doesn't like animals. I kept him at Granddad's last night, but he can't stay there."

"And what about those wounds?" Ted asked in a quiet voice.

Paula gave Jack a scared look. *Her parents obviously don't know everything she gets up to either*, he thought. So he gave a short account of being bombed, leaving Paula out.

"Doesn't your mother worry about you riding around all night in the Blitz?" asked Rose in a shocked voice.

Jack looked around the table, and for the first time he could see something in the eyes of this family that he saw on his first day with Paula. *Are they hiding something?* he wondered. *Like spies?*

Paula broke the short silence. "Jack hasn't told his parents. They wouldn't understand. Jack knows how to keep a secret."

"I knew it!" burst out Becky as if she couldn't keep silent any longer. "You see, I told you so, Paula, and there you were dragging me away from Ned and yelling at me because I nearly let the cat out of the bag saying it's *Shabbos* and you were completely and utterly and absolutely wrong, because Jack's on our side!"

She threw out her hands palms up, and everyone burst into laughter. Rip gave a couple of short barks, and Becky fed him an apple that he crunched down in seconds. The tension in the room seemed to melt away.

Maybe that's Becky's job in this family, Jack thought, as he grinned too. *Cheering them all up after their brother's rotten death.*

Even Paula's face had relaxed, although you couldn't say she was actually smiling.

"What did you think of our bread, Jack?" asked Ted.

Strange question, thought Jack. *And why does he call it* our bread?

But he nodded and said, "Very tasty."

"It is challah."

Jack looked toward the end of the table where the young woman with the foreign-sounding name—Was it Gerda?—was speaking.

"We are Jewish, and this bread is only for *Shabbos,* our Sabbath. Only for Friday night and Saturday."

Jack didn't know what to say. He'd never met any Jews before, and Cousin Gerda had a German accent.

As if she could read his mind, Paula said, "Gerda's from Berlin. She came to live with us in 1938 after the Nazis attacked the Jews and burnt down the synagogues."

"They smashed all the Jewish windows in the shops and houses," put in Becky, her face for once serious. "They called it *Kristallnacht*—the Night of Broken Glass."

"Papa was killed," continued Gerda, her voice as flat as Paula's. "They broke down the apartment door and shot him in the living room where we were reading after dinner."

Jack was horrified. *Her father killed in front of her!*

"Fortunately, Gerda escaped to England and now she lives with us," said Ted in a kind voice.

"My dad says the Jews are having a rotten time all over Europe," said Jack, glad to have something useful to contribute.

"And pretty soon, here too!" said Paula, her eyes flashing with anger again as she fiddled with the pocket of her battle jacket, pulling out the whistle.

"Why do you have to wear that thing in the house?" said her mother, clattering plates together.

"Women should wear utilitarian clothing now," growled Paula. "Like soldiers, we have to be ready for the invasion."

"What invasion?" said Jack.

"Now, now, don't exaggerate, girl," said Ted in his tired voice, shaking his head toward Paula.

But Paula glared back saying, "You know what will happen, Dad. Why pretend anymore? When the Nazis invade, it'll be the Jews who'll be the first to be rounded up and sent to concentration camps. Just like Gerda said happened in Germany and Poland and everywhere the Nazis invaded. We mustn't tell anyone we're Jewish, or they'll give us away first chance they get."

"Well, that's not at all certain," said Rose in her quiet voice. "But we've told the girls to keep a low profile, Jack. It doesn't hurt." The worry lines around her mouth seemed to deepen. "I have family in Holland. Since the Nazis invaded, I've heard nothing from them." She looked over at her husband, who pursed his lips, turning a knife over and over in his hand.

"Do you have Jewish friends from school?" asked the doctor, his eyes on Jack.

"No." Jack lowered his eyes. He'd never met anyone Jewish before.

"So you have now," chipped in Becky with a grin. "Some people think we have horns, did you know that? And that we practice black magic in synagogue and even—"

"Oh, do shut up," growled Paula. "Jack knows how to keep a secret."

"It's not exactly a secret," said Ted, with his tired smile. "Don't be so dramatic."

Paula threw down the piece of bread she was holding and said, "When are you going to take this war seriously!"

"I do," said her father. "Every single day, removing shrapnel from the eyes of children and treating old women with terrible burns. Everyone's scared, Paula, not just the Jews."

"I'm the eldest and it's my responsib—"

"No, you're not!" cried out Becky. "Joe's the eldest."

"Joe's dead!"

There was an awkward silence. Jack wished the ground would open up and swallow him. Rip hunkered down at his feet, his nose resting on his paws, his large brown eyes half closed.

Then Rose gave a sigh and said, "What sort of a breakfast to offer our guest, all this talk of secrets and camps. I'm sorry, Jack. Let me make you another egg."

Jack shook his head and pushed his chair back. He stood up and gripped the rough hair along Rip's neck. "I think we should go. But I just want to say, it's my job to keep people safe in this war. You can rely on me. I won't raise your profile, or anything."

"See. I told you so," said Becky as she gave Paula a smirk.

Paula snorted back.

"Now," Becky went on, commanding all the attention, "I have a completely brilliant idea. Why don't *we* look after Rip? We've got plenty of room here, he can go in the cellar with us when there's a raid and—"

"No." Jack cut in. "Please don't worry, it's too much—"

But Rose interrupted him with a smile that lit her face up. "It would be our pleasure, Jack.

"Good idea," muttered Paula, and she nodded toward Jack.

"Well, if you're sure; and I'll bring him food and take him out all day with me," said Jack.

"That's settled then," said Ted. He stood up and reached out a hand.

Jack shook it and it felt so grown up.

"You take care out on the streets in those raids," said Ted. "Come round in a couple of days and I'll take your stitches out."

7.

Rip to the Rescue

It was past twelve on a clear, cold October day, a week after Jack had found Rip. Leaves were falling from the trees and layering a soft red and yellow carpet over the ground, covering up the shrapnel and broken glass scattered everywhere after the raids.

He'd been back to Paula's house several times, and her father had taken out his stitches. When Warden Yates saw him cycle up to the warden's post, he greeted him with a shout of relief. Jack was only too delighted to be back. He'd missed the action and the familiar smells burning in his nostrils.

Since then he'd been on duty almost continuously with little time to go home and sleep.

His parents seemed to accept that Jack went to collect Granddad when there was a raid and take him to the underground.

Dad even gave a grudging nod when Mum said, "It's a relief, to be honest. We don't have time to collect him, and he doesn't like being stuck down in the church crypt anymore than you do, Jack."

It meant that Mum and Dad didn't ask him too many questions about why he always disappeared when the sirens went off and then came home in the morning, tired and hungry. Everyone was tired and hungry after a night underground or in another kind of shelter.

He only hoped Becky hadn't got bored with Rip and left him stuck indoors all the time. He had no idea what Paula did with herself all day.

"Gerda doesn't leave the house much, and even then, she just pops to the shops and hurries back," Paula had told Jack. "She's scared of being arrested."

"Why would that happen?"

"That's what the Nazis do. That's why we Jews must be prepared for when it happens here."

Jack hadn't said anything. It was hard to argue with Paula—she didn't even listen to her own father. But he couldn't help wondering what she meant by "being prepared." What was she planning, and did it have something to do with why she prowled the streets during a raid?

— • —

The raids had finally died down over Camden, and he was looking forward to spending some time with Rip. As he turned into

Paula's road, he wondered whether he would ever be able to bring Rip home. He imagined sprinting up the stairs to his flat, Rip up ahead. Dad would open the front door with a broad grin and say, "Wonderful you got a pet again, lad. I always regretted putting down your lovely cats."

Jack shook his head to clear it. *That's never going to happen*, he told himself as he arrived at Paula's gate.

Paula was coming down the path, but just then the air raid sirens sounded. To Jack's horror, he could hear the sound of an aircraft engine over Primrose Hill. The raider was almost on them! The sirens were too late!

"Quick, we've got to get down into the cellar!" Paula almost shrieked in fear.

They sprinted up the path.

"I've forgotten my key!" shouted Paula over the siren, as she banged on the door.

"Don't worry, they'll keep high in daylight, or those guns on the hill will get them," Jack shouted back, but inside he felt quite scared. This was too close for comfort in broad daylight.

"Where's Becky?" Paula shouted again.

"Isn't Gerda home?"

Paula shook her head. "She's gone to the baker's. COME ON, BECKY!!"

Jack had to admit he wanted to get inside too. There was a deep rumble of engines, and as he looked up he saw a Heinkel bomber coming in low over Primrose Hill. The rattle of the great guns on top of the hill started up, rattling the windows in their frames.

"Come away, the glass'll shatter," cried out Jack.

His ears were ringing, and the air was vibrating with the noise.

"Becky! Open up!" screamed Paula, banging on the door with both fists.

"Maybe she's in the cellar, too scared to come up!" yelled Jack.

Suddenly the bomber swooped in over the rooftops, and then they heard the staccato bursts of machine-gun fire.

"He's spotted us!" Jack cried out and threw himself on top of Paula.

A bullet whistled past Jack's ear and thudded into the door-frame. The Heinkel swept above them, and as Jack looked up, he could see the black crosses on the wings. Then it banked, turned, and came back firing bullets along the road, spewing gravel, stones, and tarmac in all directions. Jack realized he was sobbing with fright and shaking.

Paula was lying face down on the path under his legs, her hands over her head. Jack couldn't hear if she was crying, and he was too ashamed of his own tears to check.

The bullets stopped, the the roar of the engine moved off, and as Jack pulled himself to his feet, he could see two Spitfires giving chase toward the docks.

"Get him, boys!" Jack yelled up, shaking his fist! "Blimmin' coward, firing on civilians!"

Jack just had time to wipe his wet cheeks before Paula jumped to her feet and joined in. Sneaking a glance at her face, he was relieved to see her eyes were also leaking tears.

Then the door flew open, and they rushed inside.

"Quick, inside," said Becky, her face white with fear.

They raced down the steps to the cellar and huddled down together on some upturned crates. Rip rested his nose on Jack's lap, his body shuddering with each crump of the bombs. Dust rained down as the floor shook. Jack felt his teeth rattle in his head.

"That one was close," said Paula, her eyes gleaming in the flickering light of a candle stump.

Becky was sitting on Jack's left side and Paula beyond her.

Jack bent over Rip, wiping dust out of his eyes with the corner of his hanky, the dog giving little whimpers. Then he felt a tug on his arm.

Turning, he heard Becky say, "Are you deaf?"

"What?" asked Jack.

"You didn't answer when I asked if Rip was all right." Her voice sounded quite hurt. "I said it three times, and your name over and over. Are you mad at me?"

Jack stared at her, bewildered, and Paula gave him a sharp look.

Then he realized. "Sorry. I didn't—er—get round to telling you both."

"What?" asked Paula.

Here goes, thought Jack. "I'm deaf in my left ear. If you talk on my left side, I don't hear anything."

The girls stared at him for a few seconds, and then Paula said, "Oh, is that all? Why didn't you say so?"

"We'll just have to talk on your right side," said Becky, as if it was the most normal thing in the world.

And that was it.

All the years of bullying and jeers in the playground, being left out as if deafness was the plague or something, and these two just sucked it up like milk through a straw.

This war is changing things in more ways than one, thought Jack.

— • —

Half an hour later, the All Clear sounded, and they went upstairs. A framed photo of a very old lady had fallen off the wall in the hallway.

"That's Gerda's grandma. Don't want her getting upset again," said Becky, hanging the photo back on the wall.

Jack gathered that Gerda was often upset.

"Let's go and see if there's any damage," he said, whistling to Rip.

Outside the air was thick with dust and the smell of charred wood, still smoking in places. Shrapnel and lumps of tarmac littered the ground, and on the garden path there was a carpet of broken glass where the downstairs windows had been blown out.

"We were standing right there," said Paula.

Jack bent down and picked something up from the ground.

"What's that?"

"Live machine-gun bullet, German."

Becky put out her hand, and Jack dropped the bullet into her palm.

"I might give it to Ned," she said.

"What for?" growled Jack.

"Oh, he sells things like that."

"You should keep well clear of Ned Purdy," snapped Jack. "He's a rotten thief. You've no idea what he gets into."

Becky shrugged and put the bullet in her pocket.

As the dust began to clear, they could see a huge crater in the road. Beyond the crater on the other side of the road, the front of a two-story house had collapsed. A water main had burst, and water was gushing everywhere, flooding the gutters. A little boy was already sailing a piece of wood in the stream.

"No more baths this side of Christmas," said a woman with a cat in her arms. "Take 'em ages to fix that pipe."

"Is that your house?" asked Jack.

"No, thank goodness," said the woman. "But I know one thing, the couple on the top floor got a little baby and ain't no one seen it yet. Reckon it's buried under that lot, poor little mite."

Jack looked along the street where he could see a very young woman, younger than Gerda, sitting with her head in her hands, sobbing. An air raid warden, with graying sideburns, was stooped over her.

"We got to do something," said Jack. "Dig through the rubble, see if the baby's alive down there."

"Of course," said Paula, buttoning up her jacket.

"Hiya Becky," came a familiar voice.

Jack's heart sank as he turned to see Ned walking down the street, his hands in the torn pockets of his trousers. Rocky strode along beside him, and when he caught sight of Paula, he gave a wave. Paula nodded back.

"We don't want your sort round here," Jack growled to Ned.

"What sort's that, eh Nellie?" said Ned with a snort.

Jack stomach clenched at the playground jeer, but Paula didn't seem to notice. She'd already started up the rubble.

"All right, Paula?" called out Rocky.

Swiveling around, Jack noticed that Paula's cheeks had gone pink.

"We're going to dig through," Paula called back. "There's a baby gone missing in the raid."

"You need some proper men to help," said Rocky, leaping up the rubble like a mountain goat.

Ned stayed on the ground whispering to Becky.

Jack saw her hand Ned the bullet. He shook his head, but followed Rocky up the heap.

The warden shouted out, "This ain't a game, lads. Wait for the rescue team."

"Might be too late," called Jack.

"Oh, let them try, please do," sobbed the young mother.

The warden hesitated and then gave them a nod. "But you come right back down the minute you feel anything shift. You could fall in and be killed yourselves, and then what would your mothers say?"

Jack threw a glance at Paula, but she just pursed her lips and moved her feet another couple of steps, reaching out for a broken plank of floorboard sticking out of the heap.

He felt the hunk of concrete he was standing on sway and cried out, "Whoa. Look out. We gotta take it slowly."

"Ssh, I think I heard something," called out Rocky, putting his fingers to his lips.

They all stopped to listen.

Jack realized he was holding his breath. After a few moments he shook his head. "We need to dig. Trouble is, where to start?"

They all looked around, and then Jack heard a whining sound. Rip was crouched on the rubble, front paws scrabbling

away at something. When Jack called out to him, Rip let out a single bark and continued to dig down.

Jack scrambled over, bricks slithering away beneath his feet and came up alongside the dog. "What is it, boy? You found some food?"

Rip's tongue was lolling out of the side of his mouth, and a bit of flowery wallpaper was stuck to his torn ear, making him look even more daft than usual.

"It's probably just a rat," said Rocky as he began to pull away broken bricks in front of him.

But Rip barked again and continued to dig at the rubble.

Suddenly everything rocked, and Paula cried out, "Look out, we'll fall."

Jack crouched down, whispering in the dog's good ear, "What is it Rip? Eh, boy? What you got there?" Maybe this dog wasn't as stupid as he looked.

Rip turned his head, his huge brown eyes staring at Jack as if to say, *How can I make you understand?* Then he licked and licked at his face until Jack pushed him away with a laugh. "All right, show me."

Rip stopped for a moment, head cocked to one side, good ear pricked. Jack stayed still too, listening, holding his breath, his good ear straining.

We're the same, me and Rip, he couldn't help thinking. *Only two good ears between us.*

Then Rip leaned forward, his thin shoulders tensed; and opening his jaws, he began a steady bark.

"Oy, watch that dog," called out the warden. "He'll bring the whole lot down like that."

Jack reached out a restraining hand when a small black hole opened in front of him.

The dog stopped scrabbling and turned his huge eyes on Jack again as if to say, *See, look down there.*

"All right, good boy," said Jack. "Quiet everyone."

They all froze: Rocky on a plank of floorboard above him, Paula crouched nearby.

Rip stood like a statue, tongue lolling from his open jaws, saliva streaming down, looking at Jack with complete trust in his eyes.

Minute after minute passed. There was a curious silence in the street broken only by the distant sound of buses changing gear over the bridge and the occasional shout from a doorway.

Then Rip sat up, good ear pricked, and gave one sharp bark.

Jack leaned toward the hole, straining his right ear, but he couldn't hear anything. "Paula, come down here. You listen. I can't, you know—"

"Of course," said Paula, an anxious look on her face as she began to edge her way down the rubble.

Something wobbled, and to Jack's horror a huge hunk of

plaster gave way and rolled down onto the street with a crash. He flung out an arm and managed to grab the girl before she tumbled too.

Paula let out a shocked cry, and Rocky came charging over the bomb site, flinging an arm around her waist.

"All right, sweetheart, you're proper safe now," said Rocky.

Jack felt a bit stupid, but he kept quiet. The only thing that mattered now was the baby.

"Silence everyone," he called out in a clear voice, taking charge. "Paula, lean down as far as you can into the hole. Me and Rocky will keep you safe. All right, mate?"

"Right-ho," said Rocky.

They each grabbed a leg as Paula edged forward and dipped her head into the hole.

They seemed to hang like that forever. A small crowd had gathered in the street. The young mother had stopped sobbing and was gazing up at them, one hand over her mouth.

With half of Paula's body hanging in the hole, Jack felt his feet begin to slip as he tried to brace himself against a pile of bricks. Rocky's face was set hard, a vein throbbing on his forehead with the strain.

If the surrounding edge collapses, we'll all fall in, Jack thought with a shiver, clenching his teeth with the effort.

Just as he was sure he couldn't keep still on the shifting

pile beneath his feet any longer, Paula cried out, "I hear it! It's a baby crying. Pull me up, quick."

As they eased Paula back to safety, a great scream went up from the street below, and the mother cried out, "My baby! My Lily! She's alive, oh she's alive!"

8.

Just a Fluke

"Where the heck is the rescue team?" called out the warden below to no one in particular.

"We can do it. Let us try," called Paula, looking around at the boys who nodded back. Rip gave a sharp bark.

The warden took off his helmet and wiped his forehead with his sleeve. Then, settling it back on his head, he said, "Ain't got much choice, I suppose."

He climbed up to join them.

The boys shifted to one side as the warden peered down into the blackness. When he straightened back up he said, "Now listen you kids. You got to think of it like a house of cards. Each piece you move could bring down another piece, and pretty soon the whole lot tumbles down, right?"

They all nodded.

The warden shifted the rim of his helmet and organized them into a rescue team, gently removing the rubble to one side, piece by piece.

The work was hard, and soon they were all streaming with sweat. It seemed to take forever to make any progress, but the warden snapped at them the minute they tried to speed things up.

Gradually the hole was opened up to twice the size it had been, and the entrance was almost clear. Then Paula said, "I can hear the baby."

Jack strained and strained. He couldn't hear anything, but the others all nodded, so he nodded too. "There she is, now what?" he said.

"Now one of you lads climb down and get the poor little scrap," said the warden.

"I'll go," said Jack.

Paula gave him an admiring look.

He thought Rocky would argue, but all he said was, "Fair enough, mate."

A mixture of pride and terror shot through Jack as he sat on the edge of the hole, found a foothold, and lowered himself in.

Once his body, including his head, was submerged, the hole became so narrow he was afraid he would get stuck. All around him were strange creaking sounds as the timbers kept moving, threatening to bury him alive. He edged down inch by inch, his heart thumping in his chest. The cries from the baby were louder down here, and then they stopped.

Jack held his breath and listened with his good ear. *This stupid deafness!* he raged to himself. *That's all I need, to lose track of her now.*

His feet touched something different, and reaching down he could feel the outline of a baby carriage in the darkness. He shuffled down until he felt a firm piece of wood to settle his feet onto. Reaching into the carriage in the pitch dark, he scrabbled around.

Where is she? What if she's climbed out? But that's stupid, he told himself. *She couldn't do that. She's only six months old, the mother said.*

"Lily?" he called out in a soft voice. "Baby? Where are you?"

But all he could hear now was the creaking of the rubble.

Where is she?

Then something warm rubbed against his fingers. He felt around and touched a tiny hand. Creeping his fingers upward, he made out the baby's face, her cheeks still warm.

She's alive! He felt himself go weak with relief.

"I've got her!" he cried upward.

He heard the cheers and a scream from Paula above him.

"Well done, lad. Bring her up. We'll grab you," called out the warden.

What if I can't climb back? Jack thought, as he froze in the dark hole. *What if I drop the baby? What if the whole lot comes down on us? We'll both be buried, and then what will Dad say?*

But he knew, didn't he? *"That useless lad of mine, can't depend on him, running about in the war causing trouble."*

I'm not useless! he almost shouted aloud.

A surge of adrenaline shot through him. He picked the baby up and pressed her to his body. She snuffled against his shirt.

"Jack?" The warden's voice sounded anxious.

Then Paula called down, "Come on, Jack. You can do it."

Her urgent voice made him smile in the dark.

"Coming," he called out.

Tucking the baby under his arm, he reached out with his free hand, found a stable piece of pipe and hauled himself up. Foothold after foothold wobbled, making it hard to keep his balance. But he edged slowly upward until he felt arms grabbing him, and finally he was out, gulping down the cold, crisp air.

Someone took the baby from him, and Jack heard the mother cry out, "Lily, my angel! Pass her down, quick, please."

Rocky was banging him on the back and shouting, "You flippin' hero, mate. I could never have gone down there, me. Scared of dark places, ain't I."

Rip was jumping up trying to lick Jack's face, threatening to collapse the whole heap of rubble.

"Steady, boy," said Jack, blinking in the bright air.

He pushed the dog away, and Rip started to pick his way over the bricks, turning to bark at Jack every few seconds.

Jack staggered back down to street level and lowered himself onto a garden wall as Rip plunged his jaws into a tin of water someone put down for him.

Paula handed Jack a mug of cold water. He drank it down, one hand fondling Rip's good ear. The fur was matted like an old rug, nothing like Salt's and Pepper's silky ears. But Rip was the real hero here.

"You're a good dog," he murmured, "a really good dog."

We can rely on each other, Jack told himself. *We're mates in a war, like Dad says about his mates in the trenches.*

"We're in this together," he whispered in Rip's good ear. "Our two good ears working like a pair."

The thought made him grin, and Rip paused for a moment. He looked up at Jack with his huge brown eyes, water dripping from his jaws and gave a little woof.

A woman came up and pressed a shilling into Jack's hand, saying, "You're a good boy. Your parents must be very proud of you."

Jack felt he'd grown at least a foot as the crowd moved off.

He couldn't wait to go home and tell Mum and Dad. He

could even ask the warden to stop by and back his story up. That would shut Dad up for the rest of the war, wouldn't it?

He felt his chest swell with pride as the turned the shilling over and over in his hand.

Becky plopped down on the wall next to Jack. The young mother and the warden had disappeared with the baby.

Jack was stroking Rip, saying, "I don't care if you look daft—"

"Neither do I," cut in Becky. "You're a wonderful dog."

"The best dog in the world," finished Jack with a grin.

— • —

Jack ruffled Rip's musky fur. *What if Rip could find another baby or even a child buried under the rubble? Now that would be good war work.*

He wanted to ask Paula what she thought, only she seemed rather absorbed with Rocky.

Then Becky cut into his thoughts, saying, "You deserve a medal, Jack, you were so brave."

There was a loud snort, and Jack looked up to see Ned standing in front of them, a mocking grin on his face. "Yeah, yeah, yeah; good old Nellie."

"Shut up, Purdy," snapped Jack, the old playground fears creeping back.

Then almost for the first time he stared at Ned properly, sizing him up. The other boy looked like a street urchin in a pair of sneakers with holes in the toes and no socks, his trousers frayed and too short for him, and a grubby shirt with almost no buttons. Jack suddenly realized how much he had outgrown Ned since they were all at school together.

He stood up, looming over the smaller boy.

But Ned didn't seem bothered. The mocking grin widened, and he looked over his shoulder at Rocky.

Rocky gave Ned an absentminded nod and turned back to Paula, but it was enough.

"Deaf Nellie!" snarled Ned, spitting on the ground. He squared up to Jack, hands on his hips.

"Take that back, you little twerp," growled Jack.

"Deffo—couldn't even hear the baby, your ears are so *useless.*"

It was as though a light bulb came on in Jack's head.

First Dad and now this rotten little criminal calling him useless.

Before he could think, Jack clenched his fist and smashed it with all his strength into Ned's nose. Blood spurted everywhere as Ned staggered backward and fell down.

Becky screamed and, pulling a handkerchief out of her pocket, fell to her knees, dabbing at Ned's nose.

Rocky strode over and grabbed Jack's arm.

Paula called out, "Jack! I never thought you'd—" She stopped.

What? thought Jack. *That I'd punch a bully to the ground?*

Why not? Because I'm too useless to stand up for myself? Well I'll prove you all wrong, including my Dad and Paula!

But part of him felt a deep shame. *You'd never take Rocky on, you coward*, came a small voice inside him.

"All right, hero boy, that's enough," muttered Rocky. "Come on, you lunatic."

Rocky pulled Ned to his feet, and they went off down the street toward the canal.

Becky rounded on Jack, shaking her small fist, curly hair swinging around, as she cried out, "It's so *stupid* when boys fight. That's what the Germans do."

Then she ran off to her house, slamming the front door behind her as hard as she could.

Paula was staring after her.

"You can go too, if you want," said Jack in a rough voice.

"Why would I do that?"

"Well, I'm off," said Jack.

He pulled on the clump of thick fur at Rip's neck, and the dog fell into step beside him as he strode off toward the canal.

"Wait for me," called out Paula.

Jack didn't stop, but the girl ran up and walked alongside him, breaking into little runs to keep pace with his long legs.

They walked in silence until Paula grabbed his arm and bent to her knees, puffing away. Jack stopped and looked over his shoulder.

"So Ned called you Deaf Nellie at school?" said Paula in her flat voice.

"Wasn't just that little creep!" Jack glanced up the road, and then said in a calmer voice, "Look, we all started at elementary school on the first day; five years old, me, Rocky, Ned, and all the other boys in his gang."

"So were they horrible about your deaf ear on the first day?"

"No one knew and the teacher didn't say anything. Just made me sit in the front. But Rocky was always the biggest, and by the time we were all seven, we did whatever Rocky said in the playground. I joined in the football. Rocky didn't seem to mind. Then it all went wrong."

"How?"

Jack shook his head and gave a sigh. "I was in midfield," he went on. "Rocky must have been a bit behind me to my left. He said he shouted for the ball over and over, but I couldn't hear him. You know what I'm like on my left side."

He gave Paula a pleading glance. *What if she thinks I'm just a whiner?*

Paula gave a brief nod.

"The other side scored, and Rocky went so mad I thought he was gonna kill me. But what he did was worse. Dubbed me Deaf Nellie, and everyone joined in. I haven't had any friends since."

"Hmm," said Paula, and she bent down to ruffle Rip's fur. "Well, now you have friends." She straightened, her mouth set in a thin line.

"I don't think Becky—"

"Oh, don't worry about her," cut in Paula. "She has a quick temper, and she likes Ned, though heavens only knows why." Paula rolled her eyes.

Jack shrugged.

"She'll cool off in a couple of hours. Becky doesn't hold a grudge."

She shot Jack a look, and he held her gaze for a second.

"Becky's the sporty one," went on Paula. "That's why she's always out with the other kids, playing cricket and climbing trees down by the canal. She's fearless, not like me."

"You did really well today," said Jack.

"I was terrified."

"But you don't give in, do you?"

Paula shook her head. "Never."

The word hung between them as though it held the weight of a live bomb.

"Becky won't listen when I tell her about Ned." She gave a snort. "Mum says she's running wild in the war."

"We're all doing that," muttered Jack. "The grown-ups are just fed up because they're not in charge of the kids anymore."

"Exactly."

Rip pushed his nose between them, and they walked off in silence.

As they reached Jack's street, he said, "Do you think it was a fluke, Rip knowing the baby was down there?"

"No idea," said Paula. "We'll have to see if he does it again." She bent down to give Rip a goodbye hug.

Rip licked her face, and she wiped her cheek with the back of her hand. As she stood up, she said, "It's going round that some people want us to surrender, even in the government, Dad says. Stop the bombing before there's nothing left. I even heard people saying so and *agreeing* with it outside the library yesterday. Can you believe it?" Her eyes were wide with amazement.

"I know," said Jack. "Warden Yates gets proper angry when he hears that."

"We can't surrender, Jack. We just can't. Anyway, I'm not ready yet."

"For what?" asked Jack.

But Paula was already sprinting away back toward Primrose Hill.

As Jack watched her go he thought, *My Dad acts like he's the only one suffering in the war.*

He wondered what Dad would say if he knew his friends were Jewish.

Does Dad even like Jews?

Jack had no idea, and he certainly wasn't going to ask him.

9.

Where Do I Belong?

It was after five before Jack set off back home again. He had decided to leave Rip with Granddad for the night. He couldn't face Becky's flashing eyes again. *I'll go round to Paula's tomorrow,* he told himself. *See if Becky's cooled down.*

Granddad was delighted. "Plenty of food in here, Rip my boy," he said, feeding him the last sausage.

Jack left them in the living room: Granddad in his armchair dozing, with Rip settled on his feet.

Out in the street, Jack looked skyward. The anti-aircraft guns were sounding in the distance. *Someone else getting it tonight,* he decided. *Doesn't look like we'll get a raid.*

When he reached his flat and went inside, there was a strange silence. Usually by this time Dad and Mum were in the kitchen, the radio on and the smell of dinner cooking.

"Elsie?" Dad's voice called down the hallway.

"No, it's me."

Jack went into the living room. His dad was sitting in his usual place, false leg on the floor, puffing on his pipe. Jack could see his face was already red with anger.

What now? he thought, as Dad launched into one of his tirades.

"Where've you been, coming home all covered in dust? What you been up to? Mucking about on bomb sites, I bet!"

Jack pursed up his lips as he frowned at Dad from the doorway. "No, it wasn't like that. Me and some of the boys, we were helping after a raid and we rescue—"

But Dad cut in before he could say anything about the baby. "Getting in the way, more likely, running around in this flipping Blitz, getting yourself all blown up. What use are you to anyone? Playing with your mates and falling over like a useless lump, taking up valuable time with the doctors. I never fell when I worked on the buildings...."

His voice droned on and on and Jack just stood there, not listening, waiting for his dad to stop or to break down in a coughing fit.

— • —

Dad had told him all about his life before the last war. He'd been a brickie, carrying great loads of bricks up and down wobbly scaffolding on sites all over London.

"I weren't always like this," Dad had said, patting the stump. "I were strong, me. Big muscles, long legs, and I could carry more bricks than any of the other lads."

Jack was only six when his dad started telling him stories. That first time he'd asked, "What happened to you?"

"What happened, laddie, was the war. I were nineteen, already walking out with your mum, but I joined up straightaway. Frontline trench soldier, me, and one of the best. You ask the men round here. Then I got my leg shot off and my lungs ruined on the gas. Didn't think your mum would want me no more—"

"But she did," Jack had cut in.

Dad had nodded, and then he'd said, "You ain't got no idea what war is really like, laddie. Never want no son of mine joining up."

Dad never spoke about his injuries, but Jack knew the stump bothered him sometimes.

"That blister rubbing, George?" Mum would ask, but Jack never took much notice.

Once he'd overheard Dad saying to one of the neighbors, "They chuck you out, give you some rotten tin leg, and expect you just to get on with it."

"I know mate, tell me about it," said the man. "Shove you down the trenches for years and spew you out like so much rubbish."

All the men around them had been in the last war, Jack knew that. But he hadn't really thought much about what they'd been through. They never talked about it.

But since this war had started—*My war*, as Jack thought of it—Dad was constantly telling him how *useless* he was. It was so unfair!

— • —

Dad raised his voice now, and with a start Jack tuned back in.

"You're no use to anyone, getting in the way." Dad's hoarse voice broke down and he started to cough.

I'm doing my bit, Jack told himself. Stung by his dad's rant and feeling bolder than ever before, he snapped back, "*You're the useless one! Sitting there with your stupid leg on the floor, treating Mum like a slave.*"

"Don't you speak to me like that," snarled his dad, baring his teeth and throwing his body forward in the chair.

Jack froze. Dad's eyes were wild with fury. He'd never seen him look so vicious before.

"I don't know why I put up with you," his dad went on, his voice rising as he filled up his lungs. "Lounging around the place, eating us out of house and home, too namby-pamby to be evacuated like the other kids, still tied to your mother's apron strings!"

Jack opened his mouth but before he could speak, his father roared, "I wish you'd never been born!"

Silence.

Jack's mind churned like a bomber's engines. *Did he really say that?*

A look of agony passed over his dad's face, and for a second Jack thought, *He's going to say sorry, he never meant it.*

But there was only more silence as the clock ticked down another minute.

Jack slumped against the sitting-room door; shoulders drooped, feeling more weary than he ever felt after a night dodging the bombs.

Now I know the truth, he thought. *Dad never wanted me, and Mum probably feels the same. That's why I don't have any brothers and sisters. They didn't want me, so why have more?*

There was sound of a key in the front door.

Mum!

Dad looked up and their eyes locked. In that second Jack knew he couldn't speak to Mum about their awful row.

"Jack? Is that you? Who was shouting?" Mum called as she came down the hallway. "I've had such an awful time."

She appeared in the doorway, and she looked such a sight that for a moment Jack just stared at her, frowning.

Mum's hair was falling around her face where she'd lost her headscarf, and her coat was covered in brick dust. She started to cough and tremble.

Jack grabbed her and guided her into a chair. He rushed to the kitchen to get a glass of water.

She was still coughing when he came back.

Dad hadn't moved, his face blank.

"Don't try to speak," said Jack, holding the glass to Mum's parched lips.

Mum sipped the water and her cough began to die away.

"Raid...at the shops," she spluttered out. "I was queuing, heard there was some chops in...do a nice bit of dinner for your dad."

Jack glared at his father, who wouldn't meet his eyes.

"Heard the sirens but no one moved. Didn't want to lose our places in the queue. Never anything much ain't it, Jack, not daylight raids?"

Jack nodded but all he could think was, *I'll tear that Heinkel pilot to pieces if I get my hands on him. First baby Lily and now Mum.*

He glanced over at Dad, but there was no expression on his face. *Thinks he's the great hero after his war. Look at him now. Why doesn't he try to comfort Mum at least?*

"A bomb fell a few streets away. We all dropped to the floor and then we looked up and he was back again, machine-gunning right down the street. Six people were hit. Two dead, and the screams of the wounded..." She buried her face in her hands.

"Did you get hit Mum? Tell me."

She shook her head, face still covered. "I ain't important. Some shrapnel fell on me, that's all."

Slowly she bent down and pulled up the skirt of her dress. To Jack's horror he saw a huge red burn, already bulging into a blister on Mum's leg, with cuts above and below.

"You should have gone straight to see a doctor."

Mum was shaking and crying, saying over and over, "Those poor people, screaming and screaming. This ain't nothing. You don't need to worry about me."

Jack heard a cough, and Dad finally spoke in a quiet voice. "Lad's right for once."

Jack opened his mouth to snap back, caught a frown from Dad, and closed it again.

"Rest a bit, get your strength back, and then Jack can take you down the doctor," Dad went on. "Put the kettle on, boy. Make yourself useful."

Jack bristled again but he got to his feet and went off to the kitchen.

As the kettle was boiling, it seemed his dad's words became all mixed up in the steam and the building whistle. *"I wish you'd never been born!"*

Where do I really belong? Jack wondered.

A sudden thought came to him. *Everyone wanted the war to end, and who could blame them. But what will happen to me after the war? Who will Jack Castle be if he's not in the messengers, braving the Blitz like a hero and saving babies buried alive? I'm not wanted at home, am I?*

— • —

Jack was too busy for the rest of the day to brood. Once Mum had had her tea and a rest, they set off for the hospital.

All around them people were talking about the Heinkel bomber, shooting women and children in the street.

Jack overheard someone say, "It's all the bloomin' army's fault. They parked some lorries back of England's Lane and that bloomin' pilot spotted them. That's why he kept circling and firing. Who parks army lorries in the middle of civilians in a war? I ask you!"

They had to wait hours at the hospital, and Mum dozed off on the bench.

Finally a doctor called them in and said, "Once we've treated the burn and stitched those cuts, you'll have to stay off your feet for a few days, Mrs. Castle. That strapping lad of yours can take care of you." He nodded to Jack, who nodded back.

"I'm making tea, and you're gonna lie down," Jack told Mum in a firm voice.

Mum lay back and submitted to the treatment, but on the way home she said, "I heard you and your dad rowing as I turned the key in the lock. What was that all about?"

"Nothing," he said.

But those words—*"wish you'd never been born"*—went on burning a hole inside him as if the Heinkel pilot had found his target, a huge grin on his smug face.

— • —

Back home they all sat in the kitchen in silence listening to the radio as Jack made toast and warmed up the soup Mum had made that morning. Mum had her bad leg up on a chair and was dozing off. Dad sat grim faced, staring at the paper, not even turning the pages.

Jack felt he could cut the air with a knife. He found himself praying for a night raid over Camden so he could dump Mum and Dad in the shelter and ride off to the warden's post.

The newscaster was talking about the last night's raids. *"...And over the East End warehouses are burning for a thousand yards along the docks. Water is being pumped almost continuously from the Thames...."*

They listened in silence to the daily litany of death and destruction, and then the evening concert started.

"How much longer they gonna keep this up?" growled Dad, stirring sugar in his tea.

"Warden Yates says—" started Jack.

But Dad cut him off, "All right, all right. I don't need to know what that chump thinks about. I suppose you think I'm a right useless so and so, can't even be an ARP Warden."

"I'm going to read in my room," muttered Jack and pushed

his chair back. Mum opened her eyes for a moment, but he walked away in despair.

Jack lay on his bed staring at the ceiling, picking out the cracks that looked like Salt's uneven ears sticking up. Dad's words rang in his ears: *"I wish you'd never been born!"*

Where do I belong? he asked himself over and over.

10.

They Shoot Looters, Don't They?

It wasn't hard to make up with Becky.

Jack arrived with Rip the next morning, and the girl threw herself on the dog, dragging him into the kitchen.

"I've got a big breakfast for you, my darling," she cried out, opening a can of pet food and setting the bowl down in front of the dog.

Paula was sitting at the kitchen table, and she exchanged raised eyebrows with Jack.

As Rip wolfed his breakfast, Becky said, "Oh look, he's starving, just like—"

She stopped and looked over at Jack.

"Who?" asked Jack.

"Doesn't matter."

"Where'd you get proper dog food?" asked Jack, staring at Rip's bowl.

Becky shrugged and pushed the bowl a bit nearer to Rip's jaws with her foot.

"Becky?" said Paula, who was sitting at the kitchen table.

"Ned got it for me. He knows—"

"You're kidding!" spluttered Jack.

"Listen!" shouted Becky in a fury. Then in a calmer voice she went on, "Ned knows a man who *used* to have a dog and it ran away, and he doesn't need his dog food anymore, so he gave me some. All completely honest."

"Nothing honest about Ned Purdy," growled Jack.

"You don't know anything about him," said Becky.

"Nor care!"

Jack glanced over at Paula, who frowned at her sister and said, "I'm keeping an eye on your friend Ned."

Becky snorted and tossed the curls off her shoulders. "I'm taking Rip out for a walk, all right?"

"Well, stay near the house," said Jack. "If the sirens go off, I need him with me. Maybe he can find someone else buried alive."

Becky grabbed her coat and rushed out, calling to Rip who trotted off beside her as if they'd always been a team.

Jack couldn't help feeling a pang of jealousy. *Would Rip go with anyone who fed him? Even Ned-flippin'-Purdy?*

"Becky does whatever she wants these days," said Paula in her flat voice. "Mum and Dad don't seem to notice, and Gerda spends all day reading and knitting." She gave a snort.

Jack shrugged and said, "I have to do the shopping for Mum. Want to come?"

"Can't," said Paula. "Busy."

"What with?"

But Paula didn't answer.

As he set off to the High Street, Mum's list in his pocket, Jack wondered what kept Paula so busy. She seemed to be someone with so many secrets. *Even more than I have*, he told himself.

— • —

Looking after Mum and doing all the jobs took until the evening when, sure enough, just as they were eating dinner, the sirens sounded. Leaving Mum and Dad to make their way to the church crypt, Jack raced off to Granddad's to collect his uniform and pass him over to Charlie and his mum, who were going to the underground. Then he went to Paula's to collect Rip.

As he rode to the warden's post, bombs already falling over Holborn, Jack couldn't help noticing how Rip had no trouble keeping up with the bike. *It's all that pet food from Ned*, he thought.

Jack had no doubt that Ned stole everything he could and was worming his way into Becky's good graces with pet food and sweets. But why?

Must be something underhanded, he decided, ducking his head as a shower of splinters flew through the air from a shattered building.

As if I haven't got enough to worry about. Mum injured and Dad—he couldn't think of his dad without wanting to hit something—*and now we're short of messenger boys, and I'm needed more than ever.*

— • —

Jack ran message after message between Camden and Holborn, the streets thick with smoke and the bittersweet smell of cordite from exploded bombs, Rip running at his side, tongue lolling out of his mouth.

In Russell Square, where the fire hoses crisscrossed the road like great serpents, Rip paused to lap from the water flowing down the gutter. The puddles spreading over the pavement were too hot to drink.

Jack drank from a burst water main before whistling to Rip and pulling his handkerchief back over his face. His overalls were soaked from the spray of hoses pouring water over the tall buildings.

The dog raised his head, but instead of trotting over to Jack, he stopped, good ear pricked up.

"What is it, boy?" called Jack.

A wall crashed down behind him, and Jack jumped, covering his head as rubble fell all around.

A fire was spreading on the opposite side of the road, timbers crackling as they blazed. Flames licked up into the dark sky. The searchlights were glinting on the side of a barrage balloon floating in the sky—*Like a huge silver elephant*, Jack always thought.

The barrage balloons had appeared in the London sky almost as soon as war was declared. Floating a thousand feet above the ground, they were anchored with huge ropes. Once Jack saw one careering around the sky, having broken loose. The balloons were supposed to protect London, forcing the bombers to fly above them, but they didn't seem to be very effective.

Firemen were shouting to one another now and training their hoses on the new fire. Jack looked around for Rip, who was still barking. The dog leapt a low garden wall and crouched in front of a caved-in window, barking and barking.

Jack stared at the dog. Was he doing it again? Finding someone alive?

"Hey! What's your dog up to?" It was a man from one of the rescue teams, searching for survivors.

"Over here," called Jack. "I think he's found someone."

The man came over, and Rip pawed away at the brick, tongue lolling out of the side of his mouth.

"Worth a look," said another man, calling the others over.

Jack stood back as the rescue team heaved a window frame out of the way and pulled at the broken brick wall.

Suddenly one of them shouted, "There! It's a kiddie. Steady as you go, boys."

Rip stepped away, and Jack could see the head and shoulders of a boy, maybe nine years old, face down covered in brick dust.

"He's unconscious but he's alive. Bring the stretcher!"

Two men ran over, and they pulled the boy out, placed him on the stretcher, and carried him over to a waiting ambulance.

"Will he live?" Jack asked one of the rescue team.

"Should do, thanks to your dog," said the man, patting Rip's head. "Take good care of him. We're going to need him in this war."

Jack felt his chest burst with pride. He'd found Rip, and now they were a proper rescue team.

"You've found two, boy," he said, patting Rip's matted fur. "You can find anyone now. I'll never doubt you again."

— • —

The All Clear sounded around three o'clock in the morning, but fires still burned red across the horizon, and the blackout rendered the side streets, thick with smoke, almost impassable. Jack couldn't avoid all the broken glass, and his front tire punctured.

He dismounted on Skinner Street, and then he spotted movement in one of the burnt-out shops.

"Anyone there?" he called out.

A figure emerged, bent over, a bulging sack on one shoulder. Jack pulled down his handkerchief and rubbed his eyes. "It's you!" he yelled.

Ned Purdy stood in the doorway, his face blackened with soot, his eyes darting around looking for an escape route.

Jack's bigger frame blocked the way.

"Push off, messenger boy," Ned snarled, shifting the sack on his shoulder.

"You're looting," Jack said with satisfaction. "If the wardens catch you, they'll shoot you."

"They won't shoot a kid, you twerp," said Ned, and without warning, he shoved his shoulder hard against Jack.

Jack stumbled, losing his footing on some rubble, but he managed to reach out and grab Ned before he took off. There was a struggle, and Ned dropped the sack, hitting out with both fists. He was surprisingly strong and landed several punches on Jack before Jack managed to hit home and wind the smaller boy.

Ned bent double, groaning for a few seconds, and Rip, who'd been turning around and around as the fight went on, stood over him growling.

"Call your mutt off," panted Ned.

"Maybe I won't," snapped Jack, but he pulled on the thick fur around Rip's neck.

Rip hunkered down next to Jack, his nose settled on his front paws. A throaty growl still escaped from time to time.

"You want to keep that thing on a leash," said Ned, as he straightened.

"Shut up!" said Jack. He pulled open the sack, and tins of beans and sardines spilled out onto the pavement. "You nicked all this stuff. Just wait till I see one of the wardens."

"Better not if you wanna walk again!"

"Yeah, yeah," sneered Jack. But a frisson of fear shot through him.

I might be brave in the Blitz, he thought, *but Ned's grown up fighting on the streets.* Then he had a new thought. "Of course, I could always tell Becky you're a looter."

"You shut your mouth about her!"

Without warning, Ned grabbed the sack, shouldered Jack out of the way for a second time, and took off down the street before Jack regained his balance.

Just like a canal rat, thought Jack, as Ned disappeared down an alley. But he didn't care. He knew he'd hit home, threatening to tell Becky, even though what he really wanted to do was report Ned to the wardens.

Next time, he told himself as he whistled to Rip and pushed his bike off.

He'd have to take it back to Granddad's and repair the punctured tire, and he was already exhausted, wet, and starving. As

he trudged down the road, anger at Ned swirled around and around his head. He vowed he'd keep a close lookout for him from now on, and the minute he caught him looting, he'd tell a warden.

So what if they shoot him? Warden Yates was always cursing looters. "Making money out of folks in a war. How disgusting is that?" he'd say, and the men would call out in agreement.

Everyone hated looters; they deserved what they got, Jack thought.

But as he arrived at Granddad's flat, another thought crept into his mind.

If he gave Ned away, and he was shot, what would Becky say? And Paula? And what about Rocky and his gang?

Everyone would hate me, wouldn't they, and then it would be just like back in school when everyone left me out for being deaf.

He'd longed for friends, and now he had them, plenty of them. *But having friends, just like the war, brought a whole heap of new problems, didn't it?*

11.

Secret Hideout

It seemed to Jack that he had hardly a minute to himself. The flat needed cleaning and there were endless errands to run. He was also expected to look out for Granddad more and more. Mum used to do his shopping and some cleaning, but she couldn't do anything for the moment.

As he stood in line for food, with strict instructions from Mum not to let the butcher give him meat full of gristle again, Jack wondered if Becky was looking after Rip properly and what Paula was getting up to. He hadn't seen the sisters for ages.

Each morning Dad cut himself a slice of bread and cheese, tucked it in his pocket, and went off to work. He and Jack avoided each other, but Mum didn't seem to notice.

At a quarter past five, almost to the second, Dad arrived

home, hung his coat on the hall peg, limped into the living room, and dropped into his armchair without a sound.

Jack had never noticed Dad's evening routines before, but now he couldn't help seeing the deep lines of pain etched on his father's face as he pulled up his trouser leg, undid the leather straps on his false leg, and placed it on the floor. Then with two hands he lifted his stump onto a footstool. Jack didn't like looking at the bare stump and was glad that Dad quickly pulled the empty trouser leg down. Maybe *he* didn't like the sight either.

Then Dad picked up his pipe. He cleaned it out into an ashtray, picked up his tobacco pouch with the smell that Jack had loved all his life, pulled out a pinch, and filled the pipe. The lines in Dad's face were beginning to ease. With one strike of the match, the pipe was lit, and Dad sank back in the armchair, eyes closed, and began puffing away.

"Make your dad a cuppa, Jack, there's a good lad," said Mum each night, from the other armchair, her bad leg up on a crate.

Dad didn't even glance at him, but Jack saw his shoulders relax at the thought of the hot sweet tea about to appear. The next evening Jack added a slice of bread and jam, and Dad gave him a quick nod of thanks.

That night as Jack left the living room to go to bed, he heard Mum say something, and then he heard his name. He stopped, breath held, listening with his right ear in the hallway.

"...good lad...and he never..." Mum was saying, but Jack could only catch half the words.

"...he doesn't...stand the war...never...hurt..." Dad said back, but then their voices stopped.

What did Dad mean? Was he saying I don't understand the war, but he never meant to hurt me? A little bubble of hope blossomed inside. But then he thought, *Why doesn't he tell me so himself, tell me he did want me really?*

The bubble burst and Jack took himself off to bed, rolling under the blankets as the sadness weighed inside him. *Mum loves me, doesn't she?* was his last thought before he fell asleep.

— • —

The next day was Saturday, and Mum sent Jack to the cobbler's farther up the High Street toward Euston Station to collect Dad's shoes. There was a lot of bomb damage in this part of Camden because of the railway.

As Jack wended his way through the shoppers, he felt a cool palm touch his arm.

"Hello, messenger boy."

It was Paula, and she looked quite disheveled. Her hair was thick with dust and her clothes were dirty, as though she had been crawling through a bomb site.

"You been smashing stuff up with Rocky?" said Jack as a pang went through him.

"No," said Paula. She was looking all around as if afraid of being spotted.

"What you scared of? Spies?"

"Maybe." The girl brushed some dust off her face.

"Ours or the enemy's?" asked Jack with a grin.

"Depends."

"Has the invasion happened? Is Hitler coming to review the troops in Camden? Hope he likes the stink from the market."

"Very funny, Jack."

She stood for a minute staring at him as if she was weighing something up. Then she said in a low voice, "I want to show you something."

There was an urgency in her tone, and Jack stared back, knitting his eyebrows.

"It's very important. Please Jack."

"All right then."

He followed the girl as she turned down an alleyway, then weaved through the narrow streets behind the main road until she stopped at a ruined house.

She came to a halt and looked all around her. Satisfied that no one was watching them, she led the way under a broken-down doorway and into a passage.

"Paula," said Jack, "this is too dangerous."

Jack looked around him at planks and bricks jumbled all together. They could collapse at any moment.

"I know," hissed Paula back. "That's why no one comes here. This way."

Pulling open a cellar door, she led the way down concrete steps that were still intact. At the bottom, Paula struck a match and lit a candle. As the wick flared, Jack saw a shelf with some tins of food, a couple of boxes of matches, several candles, and a large bottle filled with water. As he looked farther into the cellar, he could see some upturned crates and a couple of blankets.

"Is someone living down here?" he asked, as he wandered around picking up tins and reading labels. "Nice tin of peaches. You don't want to let Ned Purdy know you found this place."

"You mustn't tell him! Promise me!" Paula turned on him and grabbed his arm as if to shake a promise out of him.

"Whoa, don't worry. I don't tell Ned Purdy anything."

"That's good because"—Paula paused and stared at Jack—"because this is my secret. My really big secret."

Jack frowned. None of this made any sense. Surely Paula wasn't a looter as well, like Ned. Maybe Becky had been looting and Paula was trying to stop her getting arrested.

"What do you mean? What is all this stuff for? I don't get it," said Jack.

"It's for the invasion."

Jack groaned. "Not again."

"No, listen, you must listen to me."

The pleading in Paula's voice was so intense, Jack sighed and folded his arms. "Go on then."

"When the Nazis invade, they'll come for the Jews, like Gerda said, and my family will no longer be safe. I'm going to bring them here. This will be our hideout. I've collected this food from home. Mum hasn't noticed yet."

"I still don't get it," said Jack, but inside he was relieved. At least she hadn't been looting.

"We can stay down here for months," said Paula. "Me, Becky, Gerda, and Mum and Dad, only..." She paused and looked into his eyes. "We can't survive alone, can we? We need someone on the outside to keep us informed and bring us food. You know how to keep a secret. I thought you might do it."

Her voice died away as she scuffed her shoe through some rubble.

Jack stood, staring at her, appalled. "Are you serious?"

"Completely."

"You really think the Nazis will invade."

"One hundred percent," said Paula, her dark eyes burning. "I can bring my family down here in twenty minutes from home. But we're going to need help to survive until the Nazis are overthrown."

Jack didn't like to tell her what Dad had said just the other night. Pulling on his pipe, he'd muttered, "If the Nazis invade, the game's over. We'll never be able to defeat them on home soil."

Jack shuddered at the memory, but he said to Paula, "I'll keep your secret. Hopefully you won't need this place."

Paula didn't say anything as they climbed back up through the house and into the street. Once back in the fresh air, she grabbed Jack's arm and blurted out, "Your dad, he's very moody, isn't he?"

Jack frowned at her, puzzled. "A bit, yes."

"My dad says lots of men were shell-shocked in the last war. It makes them moody at home, and angry all the time. Your dad wasn't very nice to me. I mean . . . well . . ." Her voice broke off.

"He's not nice to anyone these days."

"But you see how you can't tell him or your mum about the hideout, or the food, or anything. It could mean life or death for my family. You understand, don't you?"

"Of course," said Jack, but he wasn't really concentrating. The word "shell-shocked" was floating around his head.

Is that why Dad is so difficult to live with?

— • —

They parted at the corner and Jack walked away deep in thought.

He arrived home before Dad, and Mum gave him instructions to make baked potatoes and boiled cabbage.

"I'm doing much better, love. I'll manage by myself tomorrow," Mum said. She certainly had a better color, and she didn't limp now when she walked.

"I'll still queue for rations and do the heavy lifting."

"You're such a good lad, don't know where we'd be without you," she said, smiling up at him.

Jack hesitated, and then he said, "Did Dad ever tell you about when he was in the trenches?"

Mum shook her head, a worried look on her face. "No, and you must never ask him—he told me soon as he got home, *never* to ask."

"But—"

"No buts," said Mum in a firm voice. "Drain the cabbage now, please."

Jack turned back to the sink with a sigh. What could he do if neither Mum nor Dad would talk to him properly?

Mum put the radio on, and they listened to the latest reports: "...And as fires still burn over the docks, we speak to Betty Smith, who was bombed out last night from her home in Surrey Docks.

"'If you're listening Mr. Hitler, we ain't worried. Going to live with our daughter over on the Isle of Dogs, ain't we?'

"That's the spirit Betty, the real Blitz spirit...."

The newscaster droned on, but Jack had stopped listening.

Here we are in the middle of the Blitz, facing annihilation from the Germans, and all I really want is to talk to my Dad. How daft is that!

12.

Missing

Two nights later the raiders returned to Camden and Jack was back in action, relief pouring through him as he sped down Skinner Street, Rip running at his side, tongue lolling out of his mouth. He couldn't stand another night at home around the radio trying to ignore Dad's miserable face.

"It's a full moon tonight, a bomber's moon," Warden Yates had told him. "Them Nazi pilots can see everything on the ground at three thousand feet. It's going to be bad all over. Watch how you go—and what's that bloomin' dog doing here?"

"That's Rip," said Jack, taking the message and setting off before the warden could say anything else.

"Nothing can stop us, eh boy?" shouted Jack over the noise of the raid.

They sped past houses ripped open as if sliced down the

front by a cheese cutter. Torn curtains hung limp, a double bed teetered over one edge, and a broken mirror glinted on a wall, all lit by the fierce glare of incendiaries falling in the street.

A bomb fell nearby, and the ground heaved. There was a huge flash of orange flame, and Jack swerved as earth and debris fell over his helmet and shoulders. His handkerchief was pulled over his mouth, but his eyes streamed in the thick smoke swirling down the street.

In a panic he looked around for Rip and for a moment couldn't see him. Then he heard a sharp bark, and the dog appeared.

Jack pulled down his mask and called out, "Good boy, come on."

They rode on through the choking streets, picking their way around roadblocks, fractured water mains, and bomb craters. Above them the searchlights sent beams into the night sky as anti-aircraft shells exploded like puffs of smoke.

Jack hoped they would pick out his worst enemy—the Heinkel pilot who nearly killed baby Lily and his mum. Maybe he'd get shot down over Camden and land alive in the canal. What he would only do to him!

Jack imagined biking over to the canal, then standing hands on hips on the towpath, watching the parachute float down. Maybe the pilot would wave to him, smug grin on his enemy face.

I'd knock him to kingdom come, thought Jack, his muscles flexing at the thought.

The whistle of a bomb hurling to earth sounded above him, and a huge blast knocked him off his bike. For a moment he lay still, terrified he was injured again.

Maybe I'm dead, he thought, both ears deafened by the explosion, legs buried in a heap of earth thrown up by the bomb. Then he felt water seep through his overalls—from the puddle he'd landed in—and Rip was licking his face.

Jack sat up slowly and checked all over. No broken bones, just a couple of cuts and bruises.

He grabbed Rip and stroked along his nose. "You bring me luck, old boy."

Rip gave a loud bark.

Jack remounted his bike, and they set off to the fire station. He delivered his message to the men, and one said, "Shouldn't have that dog with you, he'll only get in the way."

"Rip rescues people," said Jack. "He can sense people alive under the rubble."

"Hang on a minute, you sure about that?" said the commander.

"He found a baby and a kiddie, both alive, completely buried."

"Speak to Warden Yates about it, lad. That dog's needed. He should go on patrol with the wardens."

The fire engine roared away, bell ringing, and Jack turned his bike back to the road.

What should I do? he wondered. *I want Rip to stay with me, but maybe that's just selfish.*

Back at the wardens' post he told Warden Yates about Rip.

The warden pushed his helmet to the back of his head and scratched his scalp. "You sure about that, lad? Never heard such a thing."

"He's done it twice, can't be a fluke," said Jack.

"Let's give him a try out then. We've got a bombed building near Euston Road. I'll take him over there and see if he can sniff anyone out alive. Here's your next message."

But as soon as Jack mounted his bike, Rip fell in beside him.

"Go with the warden," Jack said.

He pedaled forward, but the dog kept pace.

"Looks like he's bolted to you, lad," said the warden. "Better keep him and see if you can help out wherever."

Jack nodded. "I'll take this message, and then go round to the bomb site."

"Right you are." The warden went back into his post.

It just shows, Jack thought as he rode away. *Me and Rip, we're meant to fight this war together, like Dad with his mates in the trenches. If only Dad could see me now, surely he'd be proud? But could he risk everything to tell him?*

Jack delivered the message, and then biked around to the bomb site. There was already a group of rescuers pulling through the rubble. As he stood on the street, Rip at his side, one of the men raised his hand, and everyone stopped and stood very still, listening. The street was silent except for the crackling of fires still burning. The German raiders had passed on.

Then the man with the raised hand shook his head, but before they could all start searching again, Rip ran up the site and sat down over a block of broken plaster.

"Get that blasted dog away from here, you twerp!" called out the man.

"My dog can sense people alive under the rubble," Jack called back.

"Don't talk rubbish," the man sneered back.

"He's found a baby buried really deep, and then a couple of days later, a kiddie. They both would have died," said Jack. "It's worth a try, isn't it?"

The man shrugged his shoulders, and someone else said, "Can't hurt, Don."

"All right," said Don, rubbing a hand across his tired-looking face. "What do we do, lad?"

"Dig a hole where Rip's sitting and listen to see if anyone's alive down there."

"Well you'd better come up and help, the dog might not like us."

"Yes," said Jack. "Only—"

"What!" barked Don in an irritable voice. "Scared, are you?"

Jack bristled. "No! I'm a messenger boy," he snapped back.

The men shuffled around with grunts of admiration.

"What then?"

"I'm deaf in one ear. Not much use to hear anything," said Jack, lowering his head.

"That ain't nothing, lad," said Don, this time in a kinder voice. "We'll do the listening. You sort the dog. Teamwork, right?"

Giving a nod, Jack leapt up the rubble and said to Rip, "What is it boy? You found something?"

Rip walked his front paws forward and lowered his nose right down onto the rubble. He began a steady bark.

"There's definitely someone down there," Jack called out. "He always does this."

"Come on then boys, easy does it. You lad, what's your name?"

"Jack Castle."

"Stand away there but keep talking to the dog, Jack, until I tell everyone to go quiet."

The men eased the debris to one side as Rip moved back slightly, still barking and growling. When he sat up, tongue lolling, torn ear flopped over, there was a ripple of laughter, but no one called him a daft dog.

Jack crossed his fingers behind his back. *What if there's no one there?*

A large hole appeared in the rubble, and Don raised his hand for silence. Even Rip understood it was time to listen.

Within a minute, Jack heard Don shout out, "How many of you down there?"

He couldn't hear the reply and asked the bloke next to him.

"Three—a woman, little kiddie, and her mum. Your dog's bloomin' wonderful. Wish he were mine," replied the man in an admiring voice.

But he's mine, thought Jack. *He wants to be with me. We're a team.*

He reached down to Rip as Don lowered himself into the hole.

Everyone thinks you're really stupid because you look so daft, thought Jack as he patted Rip's head. *Like me at school because I'm half deaf. Look how wrong they were.*

Within minutes Don was back up, carrying a toddler, black with soot but crying loudly and very much alive. He went back down to help the two women climb out.

After a short time, a raucous voice called out, "Hang on, Vi! They're coming back for you, darling!"

A head appeared, straggly gray hair thick with dust falling

around the shoulders, and a woman in a torn apron climbed up onto the rubble, threw her arms wide, and cried out, "Ain't life bloomin' marvelous!"

Jack grinned at the rescue worker next to him, who gave him the thumbs-up.

A younger woman emerged a few seconds later, calling for the toddler. The little boy screamed back, "Mama, Mama!" until they were reunited.

"You saved three lives today, Jack Castle," said Don once he was back up out of the hole and they were down on the street. "I'll make sure Warden Yates knows about this."

"It's Rip we should be thanking," said Jack, but inside he was glowing.

— • —

The night was over. Jack was exhausted and dirty, and his overalls were still wet. Don had passed by the wardens' post, and Jack had a special mention from Warden Yates all because of Rip.

"Seems to me, lad, you got two jobs now," said the warden.

"Me and Rip will save as many people as we can," said Jack, ruffling Rip's dusty fur.

It was still early morning, and the All Clear had sounded.

Jack decided to drop off his uniform at Granddad's and go around to Paula's to tell her about Rip's latest triumph. Maybe he'd even get another good breakfast.

Mum said she can manage now, he told himself, as he walked up the path to Paula's house. *She can put up with Dad's temper. I'm fed up with him.*

Paula was on the doorstep as he arrived at the front door.

"Seen Becky?" she asked, with an anxious look on her face.

"Why would I?" said Jack. "Raid last night, and Rip found *three* people alive under the rubble."

"That's great," said Paula in her flat voice, still looking worried. "But Becky ran off so early this morning, saying she was going out to play. I thought she'd be back by now."

"She shouldn't be out on the streets straight after a raid," said Jack. "There's fires burning and stuff falling down—it's very dangerous. Where do you think she might be?"

Paula thought for a moment. "She and Ned meet some other kids to play cricket on a bit of ground near Hawley Road. Maybe I should look there."

"Worth a try," said Jack. His stomach was rumbling, but he went on in a weary voice. "Want me to come with you?"

Paula's mouth was set in a grim line, but she gave a small nod.

They set off, Rip trotting beside them. As they reached the main road, they could see fire hoses snaking through the streets down by the side of Chalk Farm Station. Dazed people were still emerging from the underground where they had sheltered through the night.

A newspaper seller had set up on the pavement.

"He knows us," Paula said. "Let's ask if he's seen Becky."

But the man shook his head and looked over Paula's shoulder to serve a customer.

"Come on," said Jack. "Show me where they play cricket."

The last thing he wanted was to run into Ned-looter-Purdy, but he had to help Paula find her sister.

They jogged on up Camden High Street and turned under the railway bridge.

"Over there," said Paula, pointing to a strip of waste ground. "But there's no sign of them."

They stopped and stared at the rubble-strewn ground. Jack could see chunks of glass sparkling in the sunlight. *Not very safe for running about on*, he couldn't help thinking. Trust Ned to bring Becky somewhere like this.

He was just deciding he was going to give Ned a right telling off next time he bumped into him—he was pretty sure he'd spot him again, sneaking around in the dark, stealing stuff—when Paula said, "Becky has a friend, Minnie, who lives around the corner. I think I know the street."

They walked along until Paula said, "There! Minnie's house is that one with the red door. But look...." Her voice trailed away as Jack and Rip joined her.

A barrier was blocking the street and an air raid warden was standing in the middle of the street, stopping anyone going through. A sign said DANGER UXB.

"Unexploded bomb," said Jack in a low voice.

— • —

As they sprinted off, the man called after them. "You can't get down there. UXB. Road's completed closed."

"Unexploded bomb! What if Becky's trapped?" Paula cried out to Jack as they ran off.

A huddle of people were sitting on garden walls or standing smoking on the pavement. A woman wearing a dressing gown and rubber boots, a small child in each hand, was arguing with the warden. "We've been down that blimmin' underground all night. Ain't slept a wink me. All I want is a nice cup of tea. When they gonna check out this blimmin' bomb?" She yanked on each child's hand, and they whined out for her to stop. "Quiet you brats, I've had enough for one night."

"We're waiting for the Royal Engineers," said the warden in a pompous voice. "Ain't nothing we can do until they say the bomb is safe. It's gone right down into a cellar."

The woman walked off and plopped herself down next to a woman who was saying, "...Then a bomb drops at the back of the house, brings all the windows down on us, so we runs into the front room. Terrified I was, and the kiddies was screaming. Then another bomb falls at the front, and all the front windows come in. We was trapped inside, and fires starting everywhere what with incendiaries coming down through the bedroom ceiling."

"What did you do?" asked the woman in the dressing gown.

"The neighbors heard us screaming and forced their way in. The door was jammed. They got us out just in time. Ran for our lives, didn't we? Never been so scared in all me life. Henry said he can't take no more, and he's only six."

The women shook their heads and stared at the little boy, sitting on his mother's lap, thumb in his mouth, eyes glazed over.

Jack exchanged glances with Paula and then, taking a deep breath, went up to the warden and said, "We're looking for our friend, Minnie...."

He looked over to Paula.

"Minnie Peters," said Paula.

But before the warden could answer, the woman in the dressing gown called out, "That's where the blimmin' bomb landed. Went right through the roof of the Peters' house, ain't it?" She raised her eyebrows at the warden.

The warden nodded. "That's it. All the way down to the cellar. But it ain't exploded. So move along there. If that bomb goes off we've all had it." He waved Paula and Jack away.

Confused, Paula looked around at the group of bombed-out people and said, "My sister, she comes to play with Minnie.

She's about this high." She indicated with her hand. "Curly brown hair; they go off and play cricket. Have you seen her?"

"Wearing a green dress?" asked the woman with the little boy on her lap.

"Yes, have you seen her?"

The woman pointed straight down the road with the unexploded bomb in it. "Saw her go that way early this morning, lovey. I thought she were running away, but I ain't seen her since." The woman looked around the group. No one said anything.

"You tell the army when they get here," said the woman in a kind voice. "Maybe she got, you know, stuck somewhere...."

Murmurs broke out amongst the grown-ups.

Paula, her face ashen, pulled Jack away.

"She's in that house with the bomb, I just know she is, Jack," Paula said in a shaky voice. "What are we going to do?"

Jack stared at Paula for a few seconds, weighing up the situation. He was tired, starving hungry, damp, and chilled. *But this is war*, he told himself. *And I'm needed.*

Wiping a hand across his brow, he said, "We can't wait for the army. We need Rip to sniff Becky out. He'll find her if she's down there."

"But we'll never get past the warden."

Jack nodded. "We need Rocky and his gang."

13.

Becky and the Bomb

Jack and Becky set off at a jog through the streets.

Rocky must be here somewhere, Jack told himself, ripping up stuff in those bombed-out houses, *having a whale of a time, I bet.*

There was a huge crater in the middle of one road with a battered car upended inside—only the back wheels were left sticking out. On either side of the car water poured like a small fountain from a broken water main.

Groups of people were already out with brooms clearing up the great shards of glass lying all over the road. Jack spotted a sign stuck up in front of a baker's shop, blasted down the center.

BOMB BLASTED AND THROWN ABOUT BUT NOT BEATEN. WE CAN TAKE IT!

A line had formed outside, and Jack could smell bread baking as he jogged past. *So the ovens are working still*, he thought, as his stomach rumbled again.

"Better find Becky soon," he puffed to Paula in a grim voice. "Before me and Rip die from hunger."

Paula was panting too hard to answer.

Then a shout went up ahead of them. "Look boys! Reinforcements!"

Rocky was sitting on the window ledge of an upstairs room in a bombed-out house, legs swinging, with nothing behind him. The house looked as if it had caved in. The bathroom wall had disappeared, but the bathroom was virtually untouched except for a fine layering of dust.

"Coming to smash stuff, Paula?" said Rocky, fixing her with his dark eyes.

"We need help. It's Becky!" called up Paula, in a trembling voice.

"What's happened to her?" called back Rocky as he leapt down from the building.

"We think she's stuck in the house with the unexploded bomb," said Paula. "They won't let us enter the street."

"Rip can find her if we can only get onto the street," Jack explained.

"Right-oh," said Rocky. "Ned's your man—knows every flippin' back route in Camden. Come on. I know where he lives."

Jack's heart sank as Paula set off with Rocky, but he had to follow. They needed Rip to sniff out Becky, and the dog wouldn't go anywhere without him. The last thing he wanted was to go to Ned's home, which was probably full of looted stuff.

Rocky walked at a fast pace toward the canal, turning into a decaying tenement block before the bridge. The courtyard stank from the communal toilets, battered doors standing open. Rubbish was piled up everywhere, and there were pools of stagnant water in the broken paving. Jack caught sight of a rat nosing around and reached down to grab Rip's fur. There was no time for rat hunting now.

One side of the block had been damaged in a raid and was boarded up.

"We never smash stuff up round here," said Rocky, as they went in through a doorway and up a flight of stairs. "People are proper poor. Ned has a hard time of it and no mistake."

Jack was surprised at the tone in Rocky's voice. Did he really care or was he showing off in front of Paula as usual?

At the top of the stairs they went down a long corridor with doors on both sides. Rocky stopped at the last door and banged on it with his fist.

"Ned, mate. You in there?"

They waited for what seemed ages, and then the door opened. A woman with straggly shoulder-length hair and eyes half closed, a toddler in her arms, stared out at them and said, "What do you want, Rocky?"

"Need to see Ned—it's a matter of life and death."

The woman nodded and turned around, walking back into the flat.

Jack and Paula hesitated as Rocky followed.

"Come on then," he called over his shoulder.

The flat was worse than anything Jack could possibly imagine. A smell of unwashed clothes, greasy food, and urine hit him, and he nearly walked back outside.

It doesn't stink this much in a raid, he thought. He nearly pulled his handkerchief over his nose, but thought it would look rude.

The hallway was very dark. Ned's mother led the way into what appeared to be a kitchen. There was a rickety table with some cracked plates and cups on it, but Jack couldn't see a sink. *Mum's kitchen's always so neat and clean*, he thought. He couldn't see any sign of looted food either. *He's probably sold it all on the black market*, Jack told himself.

"Ned's only been home an hour," said the mother. Three small boys had come into the kitchen by now. "He's asleep. Oy, Jim." She prodded the biggest of the children, who was no more than six. "Shift yourself. Go and wake Ned up. Tell him Rocky's here."

Jim ran off and reappeared a few minutes later with Ned

behind him, his face creased with sleep. He was wearing the only clothes Jack had ever seen him in.

"Don't like nobody coming round," growled Ned.

"Sorry, mate, I know," said Rocky, his face reddening slightly. "But it's your girl, Becky. She's gone and got herself stuck in a house with a UXB."

"What girl?" said Ned's mother.

But Ned looked as if an electric shock had gone through him. The sleepy look was gone from his face, and he grabbed Rocky, saying in a sharp voice, "Come on, let's go."

They all raced out of the flat and down the stairs, across the filthy yard and out into the fresh air by the canal.

Jack couldn't help thinking that perhaps Ned really cared a bit about Becky, but he still felt suspicious. *All Ned thinks about is stealing*, he told himself. *Maybe he thinks he can rob Becky's family if he gets on their good side.*

Rip was running at his side, giving out the occasional yelp as if he was glad to be away from that hellhole too. As they ran, Rocky told Ned where they thought Becky was trapped.

"I know that street like the back of me hand," puffed Ned.

They ran on, and as they reached Chalk Farm Station, Ned called out, "Stop here." He bent down, his chest heaving.

People were milling around, going into the station, or standing in queues that snaked along the High Road to the shops. It was past nine, and people were going to work after another night in the shelters. Watching the crowd, Jack could see how tired everyone looked.

When will it stop? he wondered. *And then what will I do?*

Ned stopped panting and pulled them over to a quiet corner. "No point in going near the street," he said. "Them wardens won't let us past. So here's what we do."

He glared at Jack and pointed to his left ear, the side of his mouth curled in a mocking sneer.

Jack glared back, balling his fists, but Paula gave his arm a squeeze.

"I know a way to that street down the next alley and through a bombed-out house," said Ned. "Which house has the UXB?"

"Number twelve," said Paula. "I overheard someone say it."

"Let's go then."

Ned set off at a steady pace, striding past the next two roads and then dodging into an alleyway Jack had never noticed before. They walked between high walls in single file, Rip just ahead of Jack, until Ned put up his hand. They all stopped.

He turned and put his finger to his lips, and they all nodded back.

Jack couldn't help feeling excited, as though they were spies out to defeat the Germans single-handed. *And all in silence*, he told himself, *which suits me just fine.*

Ned carried on for a few yards until Jack could see a

bomb-blasted wall with an opening in the middle like the entrance to a tunnel.

Without speaking, Ned crawled into the opening, Rocky and then Paula following. Jack came last, with Rip just ahead of him. The tunnel was so low they had to crawl on all fours. The walls were still warm from the heat of incendiaries dropped the night before, and the air smelt of burnt wood. It was strange crawling through the heart of the house, piles of plaster and beams creating a ceiling above them and the floor littered with vicious splinters, broken chair legs, and bits of clothing.

The house must have caught fire when an incendiary broke through the roof, Jack decided, *maybe more than one. No one was here to put it out so it destroyed everything, creating this weird hole through the middle.*

He pulled his handkerchief over his face to stop the worst of the dust and smoke, but the tunnel was getting warmer and warmer and Jack was sure he wouldn't be able to breathe at all if they stayed down here much longer.

Then suddenly they were at the end, and he was tumbling after the others into the open air. Up ahead he could see Ned crouching behind a low wall, his fingers to his lips. They all crawled on their stomachs across the tiny garden and crouched down beside him.

"This is number thirteen," said Ned in a low voice. He looked straight at Jack so he could read the words on his lips.

Jack nodded back. *He's not as dumb as he looks*, he couldn't help thinking.

Ned looked over the wall and up and down the street. Then he turned back to the others. "No one's about, but I can see the roadblock and a couple of wardens. We need to get over the road to number twelve. Follow me."

Jack could feel his heart thumping in his chest. What would happen if the wardens caught him disobeying an order to stay out of the road? Would he get expelled from the messengers? That would be the end of his war, wouldn't it?

Ned rolled his body over the wall and, staying very low, raced across the street and into the garden of number twelve. The others followed, Rip staying quiet next to Jack as they ran across together.

To Jack's great relief the wardens didn't spot them.

The front of the house was intact, but as he followed Ned down a side passage, he saw the destruction. The entire back of the house had collapsed, leaving a pile of rubble half the height of the building. There was a long narrow garden lined with trees. All the leaves had been stripped by the blast, and great clods of earth thrown around as if by a giant mole. It looked more like a battlefield than a London garden.

"We'll never find Becky under that lot," muttered Paula.

"Shut up!" snapped Ned. "We gonna find her and bring her home, right?"

"Give Rip a chance," muttered Jack. "He'll find her."

"He'd better," snarled Ned.

Rip had started to sniff around the outside of the house, but he wasn't climbing up the rubble.

"Come on boy, don't let me down now," hissed Jack.

Then the dog started back down the side passage, and Jack saw him pawing at a door. He started to whine and sniff.

"In there," he said.

Ned tried the door handle. The door opened a crack and then wouldn't move anymore. "It's stuck; rubble behind it."

"Now what?" said Paula.

"Leave it to me," said Rocky, tapping his chest. "I'm the master at breaking stuff."

Rocky went farther along the passage where a small window into the hallway was still intact. He picked up a piece of brick and a torn shirt that had been blown around in the blast. After wrapping the brick in the cloth, he gave one sharp blow to the window. It broke across the middle with almost no sound.

"Ace," said Paula in an admiring voice.

Rocky grinned back and then gently tapped the glass away, making sure there were no splinters left in the frame. "You're the smallest Ned. I'll give you a leg up."

In seconds Ned was through the window and had picked his way back to the side door. They listened while he cleared a

gap and then pulled open the door wide enough for everyone, including Rip, to squeeze through.

Now that they were inside, Jack couldn't help thinking all they would find was a house full of dead bodies. He hadn't actually seen a dead body yet. He'd seen plenty laid out on the streets after the raids, but they were all covered in white sheets, and so it wasn't the same somehow.

Rip started picking his way over the debris and down the hallway, pawing and sniffing at a small door under the stairs.

"Becky!" cried out Ned, banging on the door. "Are you there?" He twisted the handle, but the door didn't give. "Becky! It's me. Ned. Are you there?"

He put his finger to his lips, and they all stood in silence until Jack saw smiles break out over everyone's face.

"She's there," said Paula to Jack.

"How we gonna get this flipping door open?" said Ned, kicking away at it. It creaked a little, but didn't open.

Rocky tried running at it and throwing his shoulder against it, and then he and Jack did a run and shove together.

"It gave a bit more that time," said Rocky, giving Paula his dazzling smile. "But we need to smash the lock."

He stood for a minute thinking, and then rummaging around, he found a broken piece of brick with a jagged edge.

"Stand back, men!" he called out and started to smash away at the door handle and lock.

After the lock withstood a dozen or more blows, Jack was sure it wouldn't work. Then suddenly the door handle flew off and a hole appeared. Chopping right and left, Rocky finally broke the lock, and the door swung open.

"Like Churchill said, we'll fight in the cellars," said Ned. "You're the greatest, mate."

Rocky flexed his biceps like a boxer as Ned tore down the stairs, Rip racing after him.

Becky was huddled in a corner, her body pressed against a wall, when Jack arrived. Everyone had come to a halt.

Becky was pointing to the middle of the cellar.

As Jack's eyes adjusted in the gloom, he could make out the tail fins and metal casing of a huge bomb sticking out of the earthen floor.

A thousand-pounder, he thought.

"I haven't moved f-f-for hours," stuttered Becky.

14.

Breakfast

"Becky," said Ned in his gruff voice. "We have to go now, quick as you can."

"If I stand up," said Becky in a shaky voice, "the bomb'll go off."

"No, it won't," said Ned, casting a nervous glance over his shoulder.

It might, thought Jack, *and then we'll all be pulverized.*

Then they heard trucks revving up outside and the shouts of men.

"Blimey! The army's here," said Ned.

"We gotta go, Becky," said Rocky in a scared voice. "If they catch us in here, disobeying the wardens, we boys could go to prison. My mate's cousin went there and believe me, it ain't no bed of roses."

That seemed to galvanize Becky into action. She jumped up and grabbed Ned's hand. They all ran up the cellar stairs.

Ned peered around the door.

The engines had died away, but it sounded like a whole army of boots marching around the outside of the house, with men shouting at one another.

"Won't be long before they get in," said Ned. "We got to sneak out the front door and hope they don't see us."

Jack felt his heart sink. How on earth could they get away? It looked like his war was over and he'd spend the duration locked up. Dad would have a field day. He could hear his voice ringing in his ears, *"My useless son, never wanted him anyway."*

Ned crept forward with Becky and gently opened the front door. He looked out and then beckoned to the others. "There's a guard, but he's having a smoke round the back of the lorry. Follow me."

Before Jack could think, he was bent low, Rip beside him, racing on tiptoes around the front of the lorry and across the road. They all threw themselves over a low wall and lay there panting.

"Paula, take Becky and get down the tunnel; and you two as well. I'll keep watch," said Ned.

Jack opened his mouth to say he would keep watch, but Ned gave him a push. "Go on, get that flippin' dog out of here," he snarled.

The girls and Rocky disappeared down the tunnel.

Jack gave one glance back at Ned, his slight figure crouched behind the wall, then he turned and crawled off as a great shout went up.

"Oy, you lad, stop right there!" bellowed a rough voice.

"Ned's been spotted," Jack called to Rocky.

"Nothing you can do mate, keep going," Rocky's voice floated back to him.

Jack crawled on until he came out in the alleyway, coughing and panting.

The others were waiting, anxious looks on their faces.

"Any sign of him?" asked Rocky.

Jack shook his head. "No, but that tunnel's miles too small for the soldiers. They can't follow. Better get off home before they find us round here. Ned can take care of himself."

— • —

They jogged off at a steady pace, slowing to a walk to avoid any attention as they reached the tube station. Crossing the road, they all went back to Paula and Becky's house.

Paula was just putting her key into the front door when they heard a gruff voice calling out behind them, "You made it, then."

They whipped around to see Ned walking up the path, hands in his torn pockets, face smeared with dirt.

Rocky banged Ned on the back until the smaller boy started to cough.

"Mate, we thought you was done for," said Rocky.

"How did you get away?" asked Jack, not meeting Ned's eyes. He couldn't help feeling a bit of admiration for the other boy. He'd been really brave in the face of the enemy.

"Those stupid codgers are too slow for me," said Ned, his face streaked with dust. "I shot off down the road and then whipped through a couple of gardens until I was back on the High Road. Got any food? I'm starving."

"Gerda will make us breakfast," said Becky, looking much more cheerful now that Ned was safe. "Come on."

She grabbed Ned's hand, and he allowed himself to be pulled inside and along the passage to the kitchen, Jack and the others following, with Rip.

Gerda was filling the kettle. She took one look at the girls and said, "Go wash—change your dresses—now. And you boys, wash in the sink. Or no food."

She sounded so fierce, not even Becky argued.

When everyone was cleaned up to Gerda's satisfaction, she opened the fridge and took out cheese, eggs, butter, and jam. There was also a huge slab of chocolate.

Ned's eyes widened. "You got a lotta food," he muttered as Paula buttered thick slices of bread.

"Dad get presents sometimes from grateful patients," said Becky.

"No bacon?" said Rocky.

"Mum swaps the bacon coupons for cheese with the neighbors who aren't—" She stopped and stared at Paula, who glared at her.

The boys didn't seem to notice. They were too busy cramming down huge slices of bread and butter, smeared with currant jam.

Gerda dished up eggs, and Becky fed most of her food to Rip.

"You are to stop that, bad girl!" snapped Gerda. "Eat up something or you will get ill."

Rocky stopped eating, and giving Gerda a suspicious look, he said, "That's a German accent, ain't it?" He looked around the table, one eyebrow raised, but no one moved.

Gerda went a deep red and fussed over the frying pan. Becky stared unblinking at Rocky, and Paula scowled into her cup of tea.

After a few seconds of silence, Ned stopped chewing and stared at Gerda too.

Bet Ned hates Jews, thought Jack with satisfaction. *Now we'll see about his famous friendship with Becky.*

But to his surprise, Ned said, "We got German Jews next door. They light silver candlesticks and eat this special bread on Friday nights. Gave me some once. It were right nice."

Jack's eyes jerked to the sideboard where he had seen silver candlesticks before. Sure enough, there they were, gleaming in the electric light.

"Friday night is *Shabbos*—our Sabbath. We light candles and have nice food," murmured Gerda.

"Hang on a sec," said Rocky, putting down his knife and looking at Paula. "Are you Jewish?"

His face was serious for once, and Paula glowered back at him.

Jack couldn't help wondering if Rocky was as mean to Jews as he was to deaf people. He tensed, ready to take on anyone who was going to be mean to Paula's family, even if that meant fighting Rocky. Butterflies churned in his stomach at the thought.

Then Gerda said, "We are a Jewish family, yes. What do you think about that?"

Rocky didn't say anything. He looked across at Ned, who gave a slight shrug of one shoulder.

Rocky shrugged back and muttered, "Don't think nothin'. Suppose that's why you don't eat bacon, right, Paula?"

Paula gave a snort but her cheeks went a bit red again, and Jack gave an inward sigh of relief.

"Now everyone knows our secret," said Becky.

"What secret?" said Ned.

"Oh shut up, Becks," snapped Paula.

"No, Paula, I won't!" Becky stood up with her hands on her hips. "You listen to me for once. You don't know everything. It's good that Ned and Rocky and Jack and dear Rip know we're Jews." She swept her hand around the room. "We need everyone on our side, just in case..." She faltered and looked down at her plate.

"In case of what?" said Rocky.

"The invasion," growled Paula.

"Nah," said Rocky, waving his fork around. "That ain't never gonna happen. Like my Dad says, Hitler can't beat the RAF."

"When—not if—we're invaded," snapped Paula, her eyes flashing, "the Nazis will round the Jews up first. It's my job to keep my family safe."

"You hear the English man on the radio," put in Gerda. She mimicked a posh English accent: "Germany calling, Germany calling."

"That's only Lord Haw-Haw," said Rocky with a grin. "He's a blimmin' traitor. My Dad says they'll hang him at the end of the war, trying to scare us into surrendering. Everything he said is lies, my Dad says."

"Last night," Gerda continued in a determined voice, "he said, *The Jews of London are shaking in their shoes, but tonight there will be no more Jews.*"

She stared around the room, and then Becky gave a huge exaggerated yawn. "For heaven's sake, Gerda, *I'm* not shaking in any shoes. Anyway, you know what Daddy says. Mr. Churchill will get us through, and he's a friend of the Jews."

"I'll protect you, never fear, Becky," muttered Ned.

"Of course you will," said Becky with a grin. "Anyway, all we have to do is play cricket, and we'll *bore* the Germans to death. I don't think they've ever played cricket in their lives."

As usual, Becky made everyone smile and that seemed to be the end of it.

Jack couldn't help feeling glad that Rocky and Ned weren't going to be against Jews or anything. That wouldn't help Paula, who was so terrified of the invasion, she had set up a hideout for her family.

Everyone's scared of something different in this war, he couldn't help thinking. *Rocky was worried about being trapped in a tight space; Ned was always hungry; Paula and Gerda were scared of being rounded up and put in a camp; Becky*—he couldn't honestly think of anything she was scared of.

And me? What am I scared of?

Your dad, a little voice whispered inside his head.

15.

Caught Out

October turned cold and wet, but the nightly raids over London showed no signs of letting up. Hitler's Luftwaffe appeared like clockwork, however bad the weather. Since that first raid on September seventh, there had been forty-six consecutive nights of bombing.

It seemed to Jack that the whole of London was exhausted from broken nights spent on underground platforms or in damp shelters. The streets echoed with the sound of rasping coughs as the air swirled with dust and smoke.

Dad had developed a cough that left him breathless as he climbed up the three flights of steps to their flat each evening, making his temper even more ferocious. Jack stayed out of the way as much as he could.

Riding home each night after a raid, freezing cold and

soaking wet, he wished Rip was there to curl up on the bed with him and warm his legs.

Instead Rip had a blanket in a corner of Paula's warm kitchen, Becky spoiling him with treats from their loaded fridge, and Gerda listening to the radio. They all ran down to the cellar when the sirens went, but it was dry down there with plenty of candles and supplies. Jack wondered if Paula still went out in the raids, but he hadn't seen her on the streets again.

Ned was a different matter. Jack found himself looking out constantly for his shaved head and that heavy sack hanging from his thin shoulders. What would he do if he caught him looting again? He had no idea, and that made him more furious than ever at the snivelling criminal, even if he had shown courage saving Becky. Jack had become convinced that Ned's plan was to rob Becky's house when the family got caught outside in a raid.

— • —

One particularly cold night as the All Clear sounded before dawn, Jack was on a side street near Euston Station when he saw a shadowy figure enter a shop doorway. All the glass had been blown out of the windows and the door was hanging off.

Calling softly to Rip, he propped his bike up against the wall and tiptoed over. A small figure was pulling cans off a broken shelf.

Ned!

"Pack that in right now!" he called out.

Ned whipped around, grabbing a hunk of brick, ready to defend himself. "Push off, Nellie," he snarled, taking a step forward.

"The wardens are just down the street," said Jack in a menacing voice.

"So what? I'm quicker than them." Without warning Ned threw the brick at Jack, which smashed into his shoulder.

Jack let out a yelp and swayed as Ned charged forward.

"You'll be sorry!" yelled Jack, regaining his balance and shooting his fist into the other boy's face.

That'll be a black eye tomorrow, he thought with satisfaction, as Ned dropped to his knees, clutching his eye.

All around them were the sounds of walls cracking and rubble falling in the aftermath of the raid.

"If the wardens don't get you, you'll get buried alive anyway," Jack snarled down at the crouching boy.

"What do you care!" Ned struggled to his feet, picked up his sack, and swung it over his shoulders. "Move!" He landed a kick on Jack's leg and made for the doorway.

But Jack was too quick. He grabbed the other boy around the waist, and they tipped over onto the jagged rubble. Jack felt something bruise his ribs and let out a groan.

They rolled and tussled, neither able to land a good punch.

Rip was pacing around them, growling, and Jack almost hoped he would sink his teeth into the other boy's leg.

Exhausted, they both paused for a second, panting hard, and then they heard a voice in the street.

"Check that house, Harry," a man said. "Look out for looters. I'll look in the shop."

"Here goes," hissed Jack in Ned's ear as he started to untangle himself.

But Ned grabbed his arm, and in a voice verging on panic, hissed back, "No, mate, you don't get it. I don't loot to sell the stuff. It's for me mum and me little brothers. Their starving, ain't they? You seen my place, Jack. Do we look like we're rich?"

Jack froze as the footsteps halted for a minute outside the shop. What was Ned saying? His home was very poor, Jack remembered, but he hadn't really thought about why Ned was a looter, only that he'd always been a thief.

"If you're lying—"

"I ain't, honest. Got to help me mum, she can't hardly pay the rent, and Dad's been gone two years. Come on, you gotta help me."

Jack frowned at the smaller boy, not sure what to believe. *Give him away,* thundered through his head. *Might not get another chance.*

A man's footsteps sounded in the doorway.

"Please, Jack," said Ned, leaning over his good ear.

It's too late, thought Jack, and then there came a crashing sound.

"Mate, you okay?!" came an anxious voice from the street.

"Jack!" hissed Ned again.

The collapse in the doorway had bought them some time. Jack made a snap decision.

"Well, come on." He stood up, grabbing the fur along Rip's neck, and they picked their way to the back room of the shop just as footsteps sounded again outside the door, crunching on the broken glass.

We'll get caught, thought Jack. *They shoot looters, and I look older than thirteen. I bet they'd even let Ned go.* It almost made him laugh out loud.

Rip stumbled for a second and let out a whimper. They all stopped, holding their breaths.

"Oy, anyone in there?" the man called out.

Jack could see the whites of Ned's eyes gleaming in the dark. Terror turned his legs to jelly, and his armpits prickled with sweat.

I can't get caught! he raged inwardly. *It's so unfair...just like the whole flaming war.* And for a second he hated the war with a fury that surprised him.

The man called out again. "If you're trapped, shout out, let us know. We'll come and get you."

Just go away! Jack wanted to shout back. *Don't come any farther.*

They waited and waited for what felt like hours, and then they heard a voice in the street. "Over here, woman and kiddie stuck under the rubble."

To Jack's relief he heard the man run back over the broken glass and away from the shop. He was about to pull on Rip's fur again when there was a terrible cracking sound and the roof caved in.

Jack was thrown to the floor under the weight of plaster, Rip crushed beneath his body. Dust blinded him as he thrashed about, trying to free his legs.

"Ned!" he called out. "You all right?"

He lay still for a minute listening, and then he heard a cough and a splutter beyond his feet.

"Blimey, I thought you was dead," came Ned's gruff voice.

Jack was flooded with relief as the other boy shifted some of the debris and pulled himself out.

"Any damage?" asked Ned, brushing himself off. His head and clothes had turned white as ash.

"No, we're all right." Jack patted Rip, setting up clouds of dust. "That was a close shave."

Suddenly Rip stiffened, his nose pointing back into the shop, and Jack could feel his good ear prick up. They stood listening, Jack cursing his bad ear, and then Ned said, "It's the wardens. They're coming in. We gotta get out of here."

Tugging on Jack's arm, Ned pushed his way to the back of the shop. Fortunately, there was a door that had been blown open.

Out in the fresh air, the night still dark, Jack felt lost for a moment. They could hear the wardens behind them, calling to each other in the ruined shop. They were shouting about looters, and Jack realized Ned had dropped his sack.

"If they find us, they'll shoot me. I'm older than you," said Jack, his voice breaking with fear. "Come on."

Ned followed as Jack dodged down the alley and across a street, Rip loping beside him.

Jack came to a halt, looking around. *That bombed-out house*, he thought, *is that where...?*

"In here," said Jack over his shoulder; ducking under the broken lintel, he dashed along the hallway to a cellar door and wrenched it open.

They clattered down the steps, Ned pulling the door shut behind him. At the bottom, Jack struck a match and found a candle.

As the room lit up, Ned gave a low whistle. "Wow, they got all sorts down here."

They were in Paula's cellar, the one with the tins filling up one shelf.

What have I done? thought Jack. I've helped a looter escape and given away Paula's hideout. He'd never felt so wretched in all his life. *No one will ever trust me again.*

Ned was wandering around picking up tins and reading the labels. "I'll have this lot home in no time. You want some of it, Jack?"

"No," growled Jack, hands stuffed in his trouser pockets.

"No one's gonna know, are they? I mean it's probably already looted. Me mum could really do with this lot."

Ned found a new sack and started collecting tins.

"Stop it!" yelled Jack. He grabbed the sack and threw it across the room. Even Rip was startled and gave a growl.

Ned rocked on his feet and had to steady himself against the wall. His eyes narrowed as he yelled back, "What's up, you twerp?"

"You don't understand. All this"—Jack waved a hand around the cellar—"it's all for Becky; your girl, right?"

Ned stared at him for a moment and then wiped his hand across his face. "What you talking about?"

Jack shook his head and sat down on a crate, Rip at his feet. "This is Paula's secret. She's gonna kill me. I promised."

"What? What's happening to Becky?"

Then Jack told him about Paula's certainty there'd be an invasion and needing a hiding place for the family. "Because they're Jews. She doesn't think they'll be safe. But they can't survive down here alone. She wants me to keep them supplied from the outside. Now do you get it?"

Ned's face creased up as he tried to take all this in. Then he stood up and started to take the tins out of the sack.

"What are you doing?" asked Jack.

"If Becky needs a hideout, then I'll be the one to keep her safe, Jack. You look out for Paula, right?"

Jack nodded. "Right."

The All Clear had stopped sounding. Jack knew he had to get back to the warden's post and report in.

"I've got to go. This is a secret, Ned."

Ned gave him a brief nod and then they went back up outside, securing the cellar door against any intruders.

They parted in the street and Jack went back to find his bicycle. As he rode back through the streets, he thought about getting caught up in looting. He could hardly meet Warden Yates's eye back at the wardens' post.

"Good lad. You look done in. Get off home now."

The warden gave him a couple of pats on the back, but Jack felt like he was dying inside. *Warden totally trusts me and so do the firemen and everyone out on the streets. I can't be caught looting.*

He knew that the younger boy had been caught a couple of times by wardens but had managed to talk his way out of it, telling them about his starving family.

But there was nothing that Jack could say, was there?

16.

A Bucket of Water

Jack dropped Rip at Granddad's and arrived home before lunch to hear Mum and Dad's voices in the kitchen. For a moment he was surprised and then remembered it was Saturday. No work for Dad today, and no time to change out of the wet clothes.

"That you, lad? Come here!" came his father's hoarse voice down the hallway.

Jack went into the kitchen.

Dad took one look at him and exploded. "Look at the state of you, coming home all hours, filthy dirty, making more work for your mother!"

"It's all right, George," said Mum in a soothing voice.

"All right? All right?! No, it's not, it's a flamin' liberty," hollered Dad, and grabbing his stick he smashed it down on the kitchen table, shattering a plate and a cup. Broken shards flew everywhere.

"Who's making a mess for mum now?" said Jack, jumping back, shaken.

He was exhausted, and all he wanted was a hot bath and clean clothes.

"Shut that cheeky mouth of yours before I give it a slap!" shouted Dad. Still gripping his stick, this time he swiped out at Jack.

But Jack was ready for him. *I'm not beaten!* rang through his head as he grabbed the end of the stick and pulled hard.

"You little blighter!" snarled his father.

But Jack could see the surprise on his dad's face. Triumph shot through him. *The British will beat the Germans*, he told himself, *like Rocky had said in Paula's kitchen, and I will beat my Dad.*

But his father was surprisingly strong and held on, the sweat breaking out on his forehead. Then suddenly he let go, and Jack staggered backward.

Dad's face had gone very pale, and he was gasping for breath.

Mum grabbed the newspaper and waved it up and down in front of him. For a terrifying few minutes, Jack stood there powerless, waiting for Dad to catch his breath again.

Finally Dad's breathing eased, and Mum filled the kettle.

"I'll make a fresh pot of tea," she said in a quiet voice.

Jack stared down at his father, a shrunken figure still breathing heavily, body scarred by a war that had killed millions. There was that scowl that seemed to be permanently on his face these days, as if he hated the entire world.

He certainly hates me, thought Jack, but all he felt was numb. The struggle with his father and the stick was the bitter end.

He turned on his heel, went to his room, pulled out an old knapsack from under his bed, and stuffed in some clothes. Then he slung the strap over one shoulder and went out into the hallway.

His mother was standing there, tears leaking out of her eyes. "Where are you going?"

"To Granddad's," said Jack.

As his mother's sobs rose, Jack went out the front door, slamming it shut. He ran all the way to Granddad's flat, shaking with anger and misery.

— • —

"Plenty of room, Jackie lad, always room for you here. And Rip too, if you like," Granddad said, looking pleased.

He didn't seem to understand that Jack had left home for good. Granddad treated it like a bit of a holiday, and Jack didn't say otherwise. Instead he ran a bath and lay soaking for a while.

I'm never speaking to Dad again, he told himself.

Jack and Rip settled in with Granddad, and Jack took over the cooking. He'd learned a few things since Mum had been out of action, like baking potatoes in the oven.

He missed Mum of course, but in a strange way he missed Dad too.

Lying in bed at night, Rip settled on his legs, he thought back over the years before the war when Dad could be quite good fun. *He wasn't always in a rotten temper*, Jack told himself. Dad's greatest delight had been board games. He had taught Jack draughts, dominoes, and chess. Before the war and before Jack was evacuated, they'd spent long evenings in the living room while Mum knitted or sewed, the radio on, playing games.

Dad was also a wizard at making up games out of bits of card and paper. He was always bringing home a pile of cut-offs, all shapes, sizes, and colors, from the printers where he worked.

Almost as soon as he opened the front door, he would call out in his hoarse voice, "Jack? Come and see what I got today."

They would lay everything out on the kitchen table, planning a board they could create around the tube stations, or cars and buses—Dad loved anything to do with transport and so did Jack—until Mum grumbled at them to tidy up so that she could set the table for dinner.

As Jack fondled Rip's fur, he told himself, *Dad never lashed out with his stick before the war. I thought he loved me. So what changed?*

No matter how long Jack thought about it, he couldn't come up with an answer. *Just have to accept it,* he told himself. Dad doesn't want me, and neither does Mum.

But his heart was heavy as he drifted off to sleep.

— • —

One dark evening around five o'clock, as a cold October wind blew around the flats, rattling the windows in Granddad's kitchen, a hesitant knock came on the front door.

Granddad was dozing in his armchair, Rip at his feet. Jack was slicing bread for tea. He went down the hall and opened the door. Mum was standing in the yard.

She had a plate in her hand covered with a tea cloth. Holding it out, she said, "I made a bit of a pie for your dinner and a jam roly-poly." Her face was clouded with worry and sadness. "Thought you and your Granddad would like something a bit extra."

For a moment Jack stood there. Then he said in a stiff voice, "We're managing. I cook for us."

Mum stared back, tears welling up in her eyes. "We're missing you ever such a lot, Jack, love," she said.

"Not Dad," muttered Jack.

"He is, only he doesn't say so—you know your dad." Mum wiped her eyes with a corner of the tea cloth.

"He says enough," said Jack, and then before he could think, he blurted out, "He said he wished I'd never been born!"

Mum's hand flew to her mouth and her eyes opened wide in shock. "Never!" she said. "He never thinks that."

"Told me so himself, and I bet you feel the same. That's why I don't have no brothers or sisters. You stopped after me because..." Jack's voice cracked with emotion.

Mum put the dish down on the ground and opened her arms wide, and Jack almost fell into them. He was taller than Mum now, but as she drew him to her, the warmth of her body surrounding him, he relaxed for the first time in days.

Mum was talking in his right ear. "Me and your dad love you Jack, we always loved you. You were our little miracle because something went wrong for me when you were born, and I couldn't have no more. We wanted four children. But we've got you, and no matter how angry your dad gets he don't mean it. You have to believe me."

She pulled back and stared straight into Jack's eyes. "Your dad loves you. But he's terrified something will happen to you. That's why he shouts and hits out with his stick. He wants you to go back to the countryside so you'll be safe. He's terrified you'll get injured like he did in his war. Now do you understand?"

Jack stared back, and then he picked up the dish and said, "Come inside."

They went down the hall and into the kitchen. Jack

put the kettle on and looked under the cloth. There was a meat-and-potato pie, and jam was oozing out of the roly-poly.

"I managed to get to the front of the butcher's line yesterday," Mum said. "He had lamb, just a small bit, so I saved it for you both. Dad's having potato pie tonight."

"Thanks," said Jack, his mouth watering. He was tired of bread for every meal.

"Give your dad another chance, Jack. Please. For my sake. You're so grown up now; we forget you're not a little boy no more."

"I'm fourteen next month," Jack reminded her. "And I do valuable war work."

He told her all about the messengers as Mum's eyes grew wider and wider, and also about Rip and how he found people under the rubble.

"Rip keeps me safe, Mum," he finished, as the kettle boiled and he turned off the gas. "We're mates. Like Dad always said he had mates in the trenches to keep him going, that's me and Rip."

"Well I never," said Mum in an admiring voice, as Jack poured the tea. "So you've been going out in the Blitz all this time, and we never guessed. Don't know what your dad will say about that."

"I don't care, he can't stop me," said Jack, on the defensive again. "Warden Yates needs me, and Rip won't work with no one else."

Before Mum could answer there was the terrifying sound of engines overhead, and bombs began to fall around the flats.

"Where's the air raid sirens?!" Mum screamed out in terror.

Just then the sirens started.

"They're late again!" cried out Jack. "Go and get Granddad, I'll check outside and see if it's safe to get to the shelter."

But when he opened the front door, to his horror he saw an incendiary burning in the yard, threatening to set a wooden fence alight.

If that goes up, he thought, *the flats could catch fire.*

Mum was behind him with Granddad. "We can't go out there. What are we going to do?"

"Get a bucket of water," Jack said.

Mrs. Jenkins appeared at her flat door farther down the yard, a toddler on her hip, with Charlie, her nine-year-old who helped Granddad to the shelters when there was a raid.

"The stirrup pump's in the yard," she called out to Jack. "Charlie'll get it."

"Mind the sparks, that thing's hot enough to melt steel," cried Jack, as Charlie sprinted down the yard, grabbed the pump, and lugged it back to his mum.

Jack stared out of the front door, the incendiary only yards in front of him, fizzing away and spraying out a shower of magnesium drops like blazing hailstones. The heat made him sway on his feet. He turned and ran back inside, grabbed a kitchen chair, and raced to the yard.

Crouching low behind the wooden seat, he crept toward the bomb, his eyes almost blinded by the brilliant glare.

"Here's the water," called Mum, staggering out the front door with a bucket filled to the brim.

Mrs. Jenkins handed Charlie the toddler and, grabbing the stirrup pump, ran down the yard and dumped it in the bucket.

Mum tossed the hose to Jack, screaming out, "Watch those sparks, Jack."

Jack grabbed the hose, turned the nozzle to full power, and aimed it at the fence, which was now burning fiercely.

Mrs. Jenkins pumped away, but the fire wouldn't go out.

"The magnesium's sticking to the wood," Jack cried out. "It's igniting again. Wait, I'll change the nozzle."

He twisted the nozzle until there was a fine spray. Warden Yates had said that should cut off the air supply.

After a minute, the fire on the fence was quenched.

Now for the bomb, Jack told himself, sweat pouring down his face, as he edged nearer. He focused the spray over the bomb and, just as he thought it was working, the water ran out.

"More water!" he yelled.

Mrs. Jenkins stared down at the bucket as another woman ran up with a refill.

But the bomb was flaring again. It seemed to take an age to switch the pump to the new bucket and start pumping again.

"Look out, Jack," called Charlie from his front door. "Dad says some of them have explosives in them. They go off at the end."

"Oh, Jack, take care!" wailed Mum.

Sand! was all Jack could think.

"Where's your sandbags?" he cried out to Mrs. Jenkins and the other neighbor.

"Down the yard!" the neighbor cried back as she ran to get one.

The glare and spitting from the incendiary were dying down. The woman ran back with the sandbag and threw it over the top. It landed with a satisfying *plop*. A final fizz from under the bag, and then all went quiet.

Cheers went up around the flats as Jack stood up, switched the nozzle back to jet, and hosed down the fence until the glow of the fire had completely disappeared.

As Mum ran over and gave him a hug, the All Clear sounded.

"Well done, lad," called out Mrs. Jenkins. "Charlie, stir yourself, take the stirrup pump back." Charlie ran off.

Mrs. Jenkins picked up her toddler. "You saved our homes today, Jack," she said with a grin.

Everyone disappeared, and Jack and Mum went back into Granddad's flat.

"How did you know what to do, love?" asked Mum, wiping a tired hand cross her forehead.

"Training," said Jack. "I told you, I'm a valuable part of the war effort. Now you have to speak to Dad, right?"

"I will, I promise," said Mum.

Rip gave a sharp woof, and they all laughed with relief.

17.

Tomorrow Everything Will Be All Right

"That was smashing, Elsie," said Granddad as he spooned up the jam roly-poly on his plate.

"It was great," said Jack, feeding bits to Rip. He hadn't realized how much he'd missed Mum's cooking.

She gave a contented sigh. "I'll make a nice shepherd's pie for you both next time I get a bit of mince," she said as she began to gather the plates.

It was past six, and Jack knew Mum wanted to go home and give Dad his dinner.

"I'll do that, you get off to Dad," he said, taking the dirty plates out of her hands.

"Well, if you're sure, love."

"I can wash a few plates," said Jack. "Maybe I'll pop in

tomorrow morning before Dad goes to work. Have a bit of a chat."

Mum's face broke into a smile, and she planted a kiss on his cheek. "I'll make you breakfast."

Then the air raid sirens went off again.

"Here we go," said Granddad, shaking his head "Don't know what you want.... Get up, sit down...." He wandered off muttering to himself.

Jack leapt up, went to the hall cupboard, and pulled on his uniform. He could already hear the steady throb of engines in the distance and the guns blasting away, hoping to smash a bomber out of the sky.

There was a sharp knock on the front door. Charlie Jenkins had arrived to take Granddad to the shelter.

They all went out, and Jack collected his bike. "I'll walk you home, Mum. Granddad's safe with Charlie." He whistled to Rip, and they set off.

When they arrived at their flats, they heard Dad's stick tapping on the stairs and his heavy tread.

Jack hesitated. "Shall I speak to him now?"

Mum shook her head. "It's not the right time, love."

Jack nodded and gave a wave as he hopped on his bike and rode off.

Tomorrow, he promised himself, *everything will be all right. Like Mum said, Dad always wanted me really. He's just scared I'll*

get hurt in the war, like he got hurt in his war. But when he under-
stands I'm doing important work, he'll stop getting angry and hit-
ting out with his stick, won't he?

— • —

It was one of the worst nights Jack had seen since the Blitz started. For the first few hours he was the only messenger boy to report for work. The others were either injured or hadn't appeared.

"They're caught up in the bombing," Warden Yates said, shaking his head. "We're relying on you, lad."

Jack tucked the message into his pocket and turned his bike back through the blazing streets, veering around a fractured water main and ducking his head as red-hot shrapnel fell out of the dark sky. A lick of fire flashed in front of his face and he wobbled on his bike, nearly crashing again. It felt as though his eyebrows had been singed off his face.

Can't get burnt up like Tommy Shepherd, he thought, as he steadied himself. Often he felt like a sitting duck out in a raid, as if the enemy pilot was actually picking him out. His back prickled, certain that he and his bike were the target. The only answer was to ride faster and not think about anything but getting the message through to the firemen.

Rip was trotting at his side, and Jack called out his name. The dog gave a joyful bark back, and Jack felt his heart sing as his legs pumped him forward.

Here I am, he wanted to say to Dad, *fighting the Germans just like you did when you were young and fit.*

"We ain't army," Warden Yates had told him once. "We're like the Resistance. You remember what Churchill said, 'Hitler knows he will have to break us in this Island, or lose the war.' Mr.-flippin'-Hitler thinks he can Blitz us to surrender. We have to show him we can resist, put out his stinking fires, keep our nerve, however long it takes, right lad?"

"Right," declared Jack. "And I've got Rip on my side."

"That's the ticket," said the warden. "You need your mates in wartime."

— • —

Around midnight Jack and Rip came across a huge bomb site, rescue workers tearing away at the rubble. An entire row of houses had collapsed. Not a wall was left standing. The street was strewn with charred wreckage still smoking, broken glass carpeting the road, and fire hoses snaking from curb to curb. Jack caught the heady smell of gas in his nostrils. There was a cracked main in the street.

"Keep well away, lad. This lot could go up any moment," cried out the leader of the rescue team. He was a short, stocky man, his round face streaked with soot and dirt.

Jack had started to turn his bike away when he saw Rip stop and raise his nose in the air.

"What is it, boy?" he called out.

Rip gave a sharp bark and set off up the rubble.

"Oy, get that dog down!" the leader yelled out, running toward Jack, waving his arms.

The rest of the team, dotted all over the bomb site, stopped to watch. One of them tried to catch Rip, but he growled and bared his teeth.

"I'll shoot the blighter if he don't get off!" shouted the leader, brandishing a pistol. "He'll get us all killed!"

"No!" cried out Jack, leaping forward, hand outstretched. "My dog can sense people alive in the rubble. Don't hurt him. Look!"

For a moment the men stood still, following the line of Jack's arm, their frames outlined in black against a sky glowing with the fires of burning buildings.

Rip was pushing his paws forward and stretching his whole body, head down, until his nose was lying on the rubble. Then he began to paw away at the plaster and broken brick in front of him.

"That's what he does," said Jack. "It means there's someone alive down there. He's never got it wrong yet."

"Is that Rip?" a man called out.

"Yes," said Jack.

"I've heard all about him," said the man, taking off his cap and wiping an arm across his forehead. "That dog knows his business, gov'nor. Reckon you should give him a chance."

The leader stood above Jack, frowning, and then he placed his pistol back in his pocket and growled, "He's got three minutes, and then I'm sending you off. Got it, lad?"

Jack nodded and climbed up to where Rip was whining and pawing at the bricks. "What you got, boy, eh?" he whispered in Rip's good ear. "Someone down there?"

Rip set up a steady bark, pawing away even more frantically.

"Here!" called out Jack. "I'm pretty sure we got survivors down here. No idea how deep, but Rip has rescued all sorts, including a baby."

"All right," called back the leader. "Worth a try. Come on boys, let's dig. That gas main could catch fire anytime, blow us all to pieces. You, lad—get yourself and that dog well away."

Jack nodded, and grabbing Rip by the scruff of the neck, they picked their way over the site and back down to the street.

The team began the agonizing process of removing the rubble piece by piece and stopping to listen every few minutes.

Jack listened too, although with his deaf ear there was no hope of hearing anyone calling.

Then a shout went up. "Here, gov'nor!"

Craning his neck, Jack saw the head of a woman buried up to her shoulders in rubble. Her lips were moving.

He wanted to shout for joy, but instead he dropped to his knees and whispered to Rip, "You did it again, boy."

Rip licked and licked at his face as if to say, *I know, I'm always right.*

Within a few minutes six more people were pulled alive from the bomb site. Rescue workers swarmed up to carry people away—one man had to be laid on a door as they ran out of stretchers. People were taken off to the hospital in ambulances, and a baker's van that had been flagged down at the corner.

As they stood on the street watching the van drive away, the leader turned to Jack and said, "It's a bloomin' miracle. Ain't seen nothing like it. That dog deserves a medal."

Jack bristled with pride as he pedaled back to the wardens' post.

Surely Dad will be proud of me now, he told himself, *and let me keep Rip at home. He's essential to the war effort.*

— • —

Jack was exhausted by the time the All Clear sounded. His overalls were soaking wet again. Spray from the fire hoses was impossible to avoid when he was out in the Blitz. His teeth were beginning to chatter from the cold. But Mum had promised him a big breakfast, and he couldn't wait to show Dad his uniform and tell him all his stories of his work in the Blitz.

Mum's had plenty of time to prepare him, he told himself, as he freewheeled around the corner into his road.

But the sight that greeted him was like nothing he could ever have imagined.

The entire street had been reduced to rubble.

At first he thought he'd taken a wrong turn, his eyes still smarting from the smoke and brick dust whirling around all night. The street was unrecognizable, rubble piled high on both sides, craters in the road, and fire hoses snaking all over what was left of the pavement.

His flats—where he had been born and lived his whole life—simply weren't there anymore. Looking around wildly, he told himself over and over again, *It's not my street, it can't be.*

Where was the post box, and the bus stop opposite? What about the scrubby trees he'd tried to climb when he was little?

But all he could see on either side of the road were mounds of smoking wreckage reaching to the sky.

A woman was sitting on a heap of rubble, curlers in her hair.

Jack dropped his bike and stumbled over. "Which road is this?" he called out.

The woman didn't answer, just stared into space, a glazed look on her face.

He reached down and shook her shoulder. "Listen, you've got to help me."

But it was as though she'd been turned to stone.

Jack looked away. *What if Dad's under all that and Mum's turned to stone?* Tears welled up in his eyes, and for a moment everything went blurry. Then Rip pushed his nose into his hand, and the warm, wet tip brought him to his senses. He wiped a hand across his eyes and scanned the shattered street again, looking for his parents.

Teams of men were climbing all over the bombed-out buildings as clusters of dazed people stood about, many still in dressing gowns and pajamas after a night sheltering in the underground. Jack couldn't see anyone he knew as he walked from group to group.

Mum and Dad'll still be down in the crypt, he told himself, trying to find some comfort. *It takes Dad ages to walk home. Maybe there's a UXB in one of the streets and they had to take a longer detour. I'll see them in a minute, I'm certain.*

But he could feel a weakness in his legs as time passed without any sign of his parents.

Then he spotted Mrs. Jenkins with Charlie and Granddad.

"Over here, Jack," cried out Mrs. Jenkins, waving to him.

Jack raced over as words cascaded out of Mrs. Jenkins mouth, her voice pitched high with shock.

"I just found out the street got hit and I says to Charlie, we'd better get over there, and your Granddad didn't want me to leave him, so I says to Mr. Castle, not to worry, Jack's probably out with his dog and when we got here, I didn't know what..." Her voice broke down.

"But you've seen Mum and Dad, haven't you?" said Jack staring at her, his arms hanging loose at his sides. "Quick, tell me where they are."

Mrs. Jenkins shook her head and gripped Charlie to her side as she swayed on her feet.

"No one's seen them, dearie," she said in a cracked voice. "The raid came so quick. No one seen them in the crypt all night. And you know your mum won't sleep in the underground. I'm sorry, Jack, but I don't know where they are."

She let out a sob, and Granddad stood like a statue staring into space.

"I walked Mum to the flats last night," Jack cried out, his voice wobbling. "The sirens were going, and Dad was already on the stairs. They were going to the shelter. They must have gone. Why wouldn't they?"

He ran out of steam and stopped, staring at the little group.

Granddad seemed to come alive and he suddenly barked out, "Ain't right, all this mess. Gotta clean up. Get a broom, Jackie lad. Never say die."

Jack couldn't catch the rest as Granddad's voice dropped to a mutter, but it wasn't any help, was it?

Then Mrs. Jenkins said, "The bomb must have hit the flats before they got out."

Granddad sat down heavily on a broken bit of wall, and Jack saw that his face was gray and drawn. What if he collapsed too? He looked up at Mrs. Jenkins.

"Charlie, get Mr. Castle a cup of tea from those nice ladies," she said, nodding toward a van parked a few yards away where women were handing out refreshments to the homeless families and rescue workers. "I didn't know what to do with your Granddad," she said in a worried voice. "Didn't want him wandering the streets alone."

Jack's mind was a whirl of confusion as he stood staring at the ruined street.

Then Granddad's words filtered through to him again, *Never say die, Jackie lad.*

It seemed to clear his head, and shaking himself he thought, *Gotta pull myself together and sort this out. It's down to me now.*

"You did the right thing," he said to Mrs. Jenkins, and she gave him a nod of relief. "My Mum and Dad are under that rubble, and me and Rip are going to get them out. Right, boy?"

He patted Rip's head and Rip stood there staring up at him with his trusting eyes, tongue lolling out of the side of his mouth.

"Come on, boy," he said more urgently. "Get up there and find them for me. There isn't much time. They could suffocate."

He gave Rip a push, but the dog just stood there.

A terrible doubt went through Jack. *What if it's all been a fluke up till now? What if Rip can't really find people?*

And if Mum and Dad are already dead, he won't search anyway. Rip never looks for dead people.

All his pride in his war work dissolved away. It was pointless if he couldn't rescue his own parents.

Jack bent down and whispered in Rip's good ear. "You gotta find them, boy. This is the most important job you'll ever do. Please, Rip."

But Rip just stood there, staring back at him, looking more daft than Jack had ever seen him.

18.

Jack's Gang

"That dog need a drink?"

Jack turned to see Paula carrying a big tin of water, which she put down in front of Rip. The dog plunged his jaws in and started to lap fast.

"What're you doing here?" asked Jack, still dazed.

"Ned told us your flats had been hit," said Paula. "We thought you and Rip needed reinforcements."

"Ned?" Jack stared at her bewildered. *What does Ned know and why should he care? We tried to bash each other to bits last night.*

Then Becky appeared through the whirling smoke with Ned and Rocky.

"All right, mate?" said Ned.

Jack nodded back and they stood staring at each other, casting awkward glances around.

Paula had disappeared, and she returned with a mug of hot, sweet tea.

Once Jack had drained the mug, Rocky rubbed his hands together and said, "So what's the plan, gang?"

"There isn't one," said Jack in a low voice. "Mum and Dad are in there somewhere, and Rip hasn't moved. He never goes looking for dead bodies, does he?"

Granddad's voice grated across the pavement, "Time for dinner, Elsie." He was staring at the ruined buildings as if he could spirit Mum and Dad out to safety by telepathy.

Does he even know where he is? wondered Jack.

Mrs. Jenkins said, "I'll take him back to mine, make him a proper breakfast. Come on Charlie, give Mr. Castle a hand."

Charlie helped to heave Granddad to his feet, and Jack felt his heart sink as they walked away. Now he was all alone in the world.

"Buns," said Becky, cutting into Jack's sad thoughts.

"What do you mean?" asked Paula.

Becky was staring intently at Rip, who'd finished his water and was sitting on the ground, head drooping, ears flat against his head, eyes half closed.

"Rip's too hungry to think," Becky said. "In the trenches, Dad always said the men, especially the *younger* ones, had to be fed properly, and then they fought better and killed more Germans."

"She's right," declared Rocky. "Come on, Ned."

The two boys sprinted over to the refreshment van and came back with their arms full.

"We told them it was for all of us," said Ned, sneaking a grin at Becky.

"I knew I could rely on you," she said.

They put two buns down in front of Rip, and they were gone in a second. Rip ate six more and then drank another full tin of water.

As they watched, it seemed to Jack he could almost see the food traveling through the dog's body, firing up the muscles, as gradually Rip's head lifted, his eyes cleared, and he began to bark as if to say, *Let's get on with it.*

"Becky, you're a genius!" cried out Jack. "Right, everyone—we're looking for the post box. It stood outside our flats. That's where we should start."

Jack walked off with Paula, Rip trotting in front, and Rocky and Ned strode ahead with Becky jogging beside them, her curly hair blowing out behind her.

It was so hard to distinguish one pile of rubble from another. Rescue teams were crawling all over the wreckage on the opposite side of the ruined street. But it didn't seem as if they had pulled anyone out alive yet. Bodies wrapped in sheets were lined up on the ground, and a taxi was loading up to take some away.

Jack and Paula exchanged looks.

Jack said in a grim voice, "I don't recognize anything."

"We'll find them," said Paula, squeezing his arm; but Jack didn't even nod back.

How could we find anything in this mess?

They passed a mother and two little girls sitting on a broken wall, the mother rocking silently and the girls sucking their thumbs. Jack didn't know them from his flats.

Then a high-pitched whistle sounded farther along.

Rocky called out, "Something over here, mate!"

Jack ran up, Rip at his side, as Rocky started to pull aside broken bricks and plaster.

Rubbing his sleeve across a bit of metal, Jack could see the bright red paint of their old post box.

"That's it," he said. He turned on his heel and stared at the towering hill of wreckage in front of him. "They're in there somewhere, if they're still alive."

"They will be, Jack," said Becky. "I know it, because... because"—she searched about for something to say—"because my dad's a doctor," she finished, her eyes fixed on him.

"Doctors know about stuff," declared Rocky.

"Only Rip can help us," said Jack.

They all stared at Rip, who was standing square on the ground, nose twitching in the air. Suddenly he gave a loud bark and set off up the rubble in front of them.

Jack held his breath. *Has he sensed them? Or is it someone else he's found alive?*

Rip seemed to find the going very hard, much worse than usual. Bricks slithered beneath his feet until he stopped altogether and looked around at Jack as if to say, *I can't make it this time. Sorry, old friend.*

"It's really dangerous up there," said Becky.

"Has he gone up such a high bomb site before?" asked Rocky.

"Shut up, you two!" growled Jack. "He can do it, I know he can."

But can he? Jack wondered in his heart.

"Go on, Rip, keep going, boy," Jack cried out in a desperate voice.

But Rip just stood there staring down at the little group.

Is he too scared to go on? wondered Jack, his face already streaked with tears.

— • —

Looking up at Rip, it seemed to Jack that the dog stood on the edge of No Man's Land, between the German and the British lines in the last war, too terrified to cross. The trench soldiers of the Great War knew all about the perils of No Man's Land. Wounded men got stuck in there, pinned down by German snipers.

Jack's Dad had only spoken about it once, and now his voice came back to Jack as he stood looking up at the place where his parents could be trapped and hurt, or worse.

One evening soon after the Blitz started, they were sitting around the fire, when Dad suddenly said, "Out there in No Man's Land, trying to bring back your mate who's wounded and pleading for help, all you can think is, any minute now the snipers will spot you and..."

But then Dad had caught sight of Jack and Mum's horrified faces and he'd muttered, "Don't matter now, do it? It were such a long time ago."

How did Dad find the courage in his war to walk toward the guns? Jack wondered now, and for the first time he realized how brave his father must have been as a soldier in the Great War and how much the men depended on one another to survive. *Can I depend on Rip like mates do in a war?* wondered Jack now. *He's only a dog. I can't expect him to act like a soldier.*

They stood there for what seemed like hours, boy and dog staring at each other. Jack could hear the others shuffling at his side.

Then Rip's nose pointed upward and started to twitch. A little ray of hope flew up through Jack. He held his breath, not daring to speak as the dog set off up the rubble again, coming to a stop on a small shelf of wood sticking out of the bricks.

He sat down and began a steady bark, his harsh animal tones echoing around the ruined street.

"'Ere, what's that blimmin' dog doing?" cried out a rescue worker across the street.

"He's found my mum and dad, that's what!" shouted Jack.

"Well don't do nothing," called out another worker. "Wait for our team to get over there."

"No fear," muttered Rocky to Jack. "Come on, gang, we know what to do." Leaping up the rubble after Rip, he called back down, "Come on Ned, what ya waiting for?"

"All right," muttered Ned and, casting a last glance at Becky, he set off up the rubble, picking his way carefully as Jack leapt forward and overtook him.

Rip had already marked out the route for them, and soon they were all gathered around the dog. Rip had lowered his body down on his paws, back outstretched, nose pushed forward as far as it would go. He was twitching and sniffing at the area in front of him.

"We dig down here," commanded Jack.

"Righto," said Rocky. "But remember what the warden said last time," he told Jack as they started to tear away at the rubble. "Take it slowly or you'll make things worse."

Jack nodded and organized them into a rescue party, taking pieces carefully from the area and starting to drill down into the rubble. Paula joined them, but it was still hard going.

After nearly an hour, when Jack was beginning to feel the exhaustion of a whole night's work, no sleep, and hardly anything to eat, a hole the size of Rip's head opened up.

Jack put up his hand to halt the work and then lay himself

flat over the rubble and stared down into the depths. He wriggled forward and some bricks loosened beneath his feet, rattling down the mound.

"Watch out, mate," called out Rocky, grabbing Jack's legs

"I'm gonna call down. Absolute silence everyone so we can hear them call back."

Jack saw Paula exchange an anxious glance with Rocky before he turned his head back to the hole. *She doesn't believe they're alive,* he told himself, *but they are, I know they are. Rip's never wrong.*

Taking a deep breath, Jack roared down the hole, pushing his voice as hard as he could. "Dad! Mum! It's Jack! Are you in there?"

They all stood still, Jack holding his breath and listening with his good ear plugged into the hole.

But all he could hear was the creaking of timber as the wreckage shifted.

He called again and again, stopping to listen each time, straining his good ear, and then, just as he was about to call Paula over to listen for him, he heard a faint sound.

"Dad?" he called out.

A brick rolled down the mound.

"Dad?"

"That you, Jack?" The voice was faint, and Jack could just about hear it.

"Yes! It's me Dad. What about Mum?"

But he couldn't hear the reply.

"Paula!" he shouted out. "Come and listen for me. Quick."

Paula scrambled over, and Rocky held her tight as she lay down, head in the hole.

They all waited, and then she pulled herself out and said, "Okay, they're both alive, but your mum's arm is trapped."

Jack felt a great sob burst from his chest, and Rocky banged him on the back, saying, "Well done, mate, you did it. They're gonna be all right."

Jack took Paula's place and called down, "We're coming, Dad. Just hold on. We'll get you out."

Rescue workers, hearing their shouts, had swarmed up the mound, and now they took over. Jack and the others were ordered down to the street.

It could all still go wrong, Jack couldn't help worrying. *If they're not careful enough, the whole lot could go down on Mum's and Dad's heads.*

There was nothing he could do except watch and wait.

It seemed to take the rest of the morning for the team to make progress, but as the sun came out from behind dark October clouds at lunchtime, Jack heard a shout.

"Come on then, steady as you go," a voice called out.

Mum's head appeared in the hole and then her whole body, and she was actually standing up as someone helped her down the rubble.

She flew into Jack's arms on the street, and as they sobbed in each other's arms, Jack said, "What about Dad?"

Mum pulled back. "Jack, he was a real hero. He lost his false leg and everything, but he wouldn't let them take him up until they set me free and took me first. Is he out yet?"

They stared up the mound, and all Jack could think was, *How on earth is Dad going to climb out of that lot with one leg?*

Then they heard a man say, "Here he comes. Careful there. Got an injury on that side."

Dad's head, white with dust, emerged above them, but it took a while to ease him out.

"Stretcher!" someone hollered.

Two men appeared with a stretcher and clambered up. It took six of them to bring Dad back to the street.

Jack looked down in horror at Dad's injuries. His trousers were hanging off his body and his stump was slashed and bleeding. Jack couldn't imagine the pain, but his father grinned up at him and stuck up his thumbs.

"Never say die, eh son?" he rasped out, his voice more hoarse than ever. Looking around at the group of children he said, "Who's this lot, then?"

Jack couldn't speak.

It was Becky who called out, "We're Jack's gang, of course."

19.

All Your Friends

There was nothing left to do but to go and live with Granddad. Mum arrived back later that day, but Dad needed surgery and wouldn't be home for almost a week. They had lost everything in the raid except the clothes they were in, and Granddad had very little to spare.

"Only two plates and mugs, and they're all cracked," said Mum going through Granddad's cupboards.

They made several trips to a center set up in the church for bombed-out families, returning home with piles of bedding, clothes, and kitchen stuff.

"I never realized how much we needed," said Jack, searching for a can opener.

They made up the big bed in Granddad's room for Mum and

Dad, Granddad moved into the little bedroom, and Jack slept on the sofa.

The raids had died down over Camden. Each night Jack rolled under the blankets as Rip curled up on the rug, and they watched the embers in the fireplace. Jack wondered what Dad was thinking about as he lay in his hospital bed all alone.

Mum visited Dad every day, but Jack wasn't allowed.

"There's too many people coming into the wards. Best you stay away," Mum told him. "Plenty of time to catch up when Dad comes home."

If Jack was honest, he felt relieved. So much had happened in the past week, he couldn't face another row and definitely not in public. What if nothing had changed between him and Dad, despite the rescue?

— • —

On the third morning, all the jobs done and the flat finally beginning to look like home, Jack walked over to Paula and Becky's house with Rip. He knocked on the front door and waited for ages before Paula opened up.

"Becky's out," she said in her flat voice and turned into the house, Jack following.

In the big kitchen at the back, a kettle was whistling on the stove. Paula made tea, and they sat at the long wooden table, stirring sugar in silence.

Then Paula said, "Rocky told me Ned found my hideout."

Jack nodded. "He loots shops."

"I know. But will he keep our secret?"

"Of course, he's in love with Becky."

That made Paula smile.

Jack put his teaspoon down and gave Paula a careful look. "You know all this stuff about keeping a low profile...."

Paula gave an impatient shake of her head.

"No, listen, hear me out," said Jack. "I know how that feels. Being deaf on one side, I mean. I didn't tell the wardens or the firemen in case they wouldn't have me, and I didn't even tell you and Becky in case, well, in case you didn't want to be my friend, like in school."

"So what?"

"Well, all I'm saying is, even if Warden Yates found out now, he knows I'm one of the best boys he's got, so he wouldn't throw me out. You and Becky didn't care when I told you. I think in the war we have to be able to trust each other, know who our friends are, that's all."

He ducked his head and stared into the swirling tea. There was a silence, and Jack thought Paula would change the subject. That she didn't understand. He probably should go and leave her to it.

But then she blurted out, "You're right, I know you are."

"I am?"

"Yes. I've been so scared since Gerda arrived with all her terrible stories of Nazis attacking the Jews, and then Joe died, and it was like the world came to an end. I don't know if there'll be an invasion or what will happen to the Jews or anyone else in England. But I do know me and Becky and all our family need our friends. Don't we, Jack?"

"Yes," said Jack, bending down to ruffle Rip's fur. He straightened up to see a tear trickling down Paula's cheek.

Finally, thought Jack. *Maybe flat, monotone Paula was going to start actually feeling things instead of always being on battle alert.*

"You don't have to fight this war all by yourself," he said, stroking Rip's good ear.

Paula nodded, more tears escaping.

"You have me and Rip, and Rocky and his gang, and even the horrible Ned."

That made them both laugh.

"We just have to stick together, and if the Germans do invade, we'll run circles round them while Ned steals their ammo."

"Or a tank or two," said Paula, wiping her cheeks with the back of her hand. "You're right, Jack. We need all the friends we can get to survive this war."

Jack nodded and pulled on Rip's fur. "I'd better go. Bound to be another raid tonight, and I need some sleep."

As Paula saw him to the door, she said, "You look after yourself, Jack Castle. I won't be around every time you get blown up."

"Messenger boys don't worry about all that stuff," he said, with a short laugh. "Like Rocky always says, 'Worrying's for the gutless.'"

Paula laughed as Jack and Rip walked away back to Camden High Street.

— • —

For the next two nights the raiders returned, and Jack was busy with Rip, running messages and pulling people alive from bomb sites. Each morning when he returned to Granddad's flat, Mum was already home from the shelter making breakfast. She didn't quiz Jack, but she looked as though she wasn't getting much sleep.

On the third morning, Rip found a whole family alive near Holborn, and Jack stayed to help with the rescue effort. It was nearly lunchtime before he arrived back in the flat.

As he opened the front door, a familiar hoarse voice came from the sitting room. "Dad!"

He ran in, and there was Dad, his stump up on a footstool, sucking on his pipe.

"All right, son," croaked Dad. "Was wondering when you were gonna come home."

Jack hesitated in the doorway.

Are things different now, he wondered, *or is Dad going to go back to shouting and crashing his stick around?*

"I'll just change," muttered Jack, turning to go.

"Stay a minute, eh lad?"

Jack turned back. His dad was gazing up at him, his eyes soft as if . . . as if filled with a sort of pride.

Was he mistaken?

"You saved our lives, Jack," said Dad. "You and that dog of yours. Rip, isn't it?"

Jack stood there not knowing what to say.

"I made a lot of mistakes in my life," Dad went on.

Here we go, thought Jack. *And I'm the biggest mistake.*

"But having you was one of the best things I ever done— that and marrying your mum of course."

Jack wasn't sure he'd heard properly. His stupid left ear. He turned the right side of his face toward Dad and said, "Having me?"

Dad sucked on his pipe and nodded. "You, son. Yes. You, my boy."

A moment passed as the clock ticked down the seconds, and Jack allowed the words he had waited so long to hear sink through him.

My boy, he said. My boy.

"You gotta understand," Dad croaked. "I saw this war coming like all the men, and all I could think were, my boy's going to get hurt like me in the last war. I were proper terrified, and I don't mind admitting it. I wanted you tucked away safe and sound in the countryside."

He stared up at Jack, who ducked his head.

"So I got more and more angry," Dad went on. "I felt useless. There you are, all grown up and making your own decisions like a man, and me stuck in this chair with my flippin' leg."

He tapped the wounded stump, swathed in thick bandages, with his pipe.

"I ain't no use anymore!" Dad's voice rose for a second as his back arched.

Jack flinched, and glancing around the room for the stick, he spotted two crutches propped up by the fireplace. *The hospital must have sent him home with those*, he thought. But they were out of reach. Dad slumped back in his chair.

As Jack stood there looking down at his dad, a deep pity went through him.

"You're not useless," said Jack. "You look after Mum and me. You go out to work, and we never go without. This kid I know, Ned, hasn't got a dad, and his family is starving."

Dad looked up at him, and their eyes locked for a moment.

Things are proper different now, thought Jack. *At last.*

Mum came in with a pile of sandwiches and a pot of tea, and they picnicked in the living room around Dad's armchair.

"All together, eh Jackie lad," Granddad said, a beam on his face.

"Good of you to take us in," said Dad in his hoarse voice as Granddad stirred his tea around and around as if mesmerized by the swirling liquid.

"This Blitz," said Dad. "It ain't gonna stop anytime soon. We're getting thousands killed and wounded, to say nothing of the homeless."

He caught Mum's eye and she nodded back.

"Remember what Churchill said," added Jack. "About fighting on the beaches and never surrendering."

"Let's hope it don't come to that," muttered Dad.

Jack leaned down and stroked Rip's musky fur. Then, taking a deep breath he said, "Well it's my job to make sure it doesn't."

His dad turned to him, that same look of agony on his face that Jack saw that day of their terrible row.

"Churchill told us all he had to give us was blood, sweat, and tears. What if it ain't enough?" said Dad, his voice breaking down into a cough.

"It will be," said Jack. "We won't be beaten. Look how everyone stands up to the Blitz. London isn't ready to surrender, and us kids, well, there's loads of us doing proper war work, fire watching and running messages and putting out incendiaries."

"Your mum told me how you saved these flats from getting burnt down. Don't know where you get it from, all that courage."

"Obvious, isn't it?"

Dad pulled on his pipe and stared thoughtfully at Jack.

"From *you*, Dad. I learned from you."

"Quite right," said Granddad in a lucid moment.

Jack went on, "You did your bit in the last war. You were a hero then, Dad, *and* you wouldn't let them take you out of the bomb site before Mum last week, even though you had the worse injuries. You're just as brave as you were in your war. But now you have to let me do my war work—with Rip."

They all looked at Rip, who had his trusting brown eyes fixed on Jack.

"Well I reckon you're both heroes," said Dad.

Jack beamed with pride, and then Granddad banged his mug on the table and said, "Ain't there no more tea? You'd think there was a war on."

Jack picked up the teapot, and as he went off to the kitchen to fill the kettle, he sang softly under his breath, *"Whistle while you work, Hitler is a twerp..."*

Author's Note

Firstly, this is the story of Rip, the rescue dog, who had a talent for sensing people buried alive under the rubble. Rip was a stray mix-breed terrier, found by an air raid warden in the Blitz. During WWII he saved the lives of more than a hundred people buried alive after raids. He was the forerunner of search-and-rescue dogs, now used after earthquakes and during wars to find survivors. Rip was awarded the PDSA Dickin Medal (often referred to as "the animal's Victoria Cross"). The citation that accompanied the medal reads: "For locating many air raid victims during the Blitz of 1940." Rip died in 1946 and was buried in the PDSA Ilford Animal Cemetery in London.

The second story that caught my eye was about the teenage messenger boys who biked through the Blitz in London and all the major cities, with messages for the fire stations when the telephone wires went down. Some of these boys lied about their ages and were much younger that the official age of seventeen.

I therefore decided to set my next book in the Blitz and to highlight the work of children and animals to show how brave and important both were to the war effort. People had put down their pets at the beginning of WWII, thinking they would go mad and bite people in the Blitz and be a drain on resources. But my research showed that many animals survived the war and in fact were a great help to their owners, sometimes even saving their lives.

Ned's story is based on the extraordinary seven-year-old, Fred Rowe, who stayed above ground during the Blitz to be first into the shops to loot food for his starving family. When his mum said, "They shoot looters," Fred scoffed, "They won't shoot a seven-year-old."

The story of the evacuation of millions of children from our cities because of the war is well known, but there were also many brave children and animals that made a valuable contribution to the war effort, and their stories need to be told too.

Miriam Halahmy